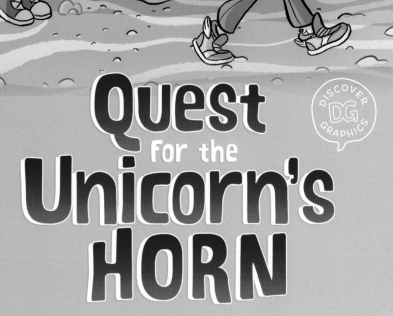

Quest for the Unicorn's HORN

WRITTEN BY ELIZABETH PAGEL-HOGAN

ILLUSTRATED BY ROMAN DÍAZ

PICTURE WINDOW BOOKS
a capstone imprint

Discover Graphics is published by Picture Window Books,
an imprint of Capstone.
1710 Roe Crest Drive
North Mankato, Minnesota 56003
www.capstonepub.com

Library of Congress Cataloging-in-Publication Data
Names: Pagel-Hogan, Elizabeth, author. | Diaz, Roman, illustrator.
Title: Quest for the unicorn's horn / by Elizabeth Pagel-Hogan ;
    illustrated by Roman Diaz.
Description: North Mankato, Minnesota : Picture Window Books,
    a Capstone imprint, [2021] | Series: Discover graphics. Mythical
    creatures | Audience: Ages 5–7. | Audience: Grades K–1.
Identifiers: LCCN 2020031503 (print) | LCCN 2020031504 (ebook) |
    ISBN 9781515882060 (hardcover) | ISBN 9781515883111 (paperback) |
    ISBN 9781515892199 (eBook PDF) | ISBN 9781515892625 (kindle edition)
Subjects: LCSH: Graphic novels. | CYAC: Graphic novels. | Unicorns—
    Fiction. | Candy—Fiction. | Adventure and adventurers—Fiction.
Classification: LCC PZ7.7.P13 Qu 2021 (print) | LCC PZ7.7.P13 (ebook) |
    DDC 741.5/973—dc23
LC record available at https://lccn.loc.gov/2020031503
LC ebook record available at https://lccn.loc.gov/2020031504

Summary: A taste for sweets and adventure leads Michael on a quest to
find a unicorn's lost horn. Will Michael and the unicorn survive Sweetlandia
long enough to retrieve the colorful, sugarcoated prize?

Editorial Credits:
Editor: Mari Bolte; Designer: Kay Fraser; Media Researcher: Tracy Cummins;
Production Specialist: Katy LaVigne

WORDS TO KNOW

destiny—a special purpose

guardian—someone who specially
watches and protects something

quest—an adventure in which a
hero tries to achieve a goal

Printed and bound in the USA. PO 3837

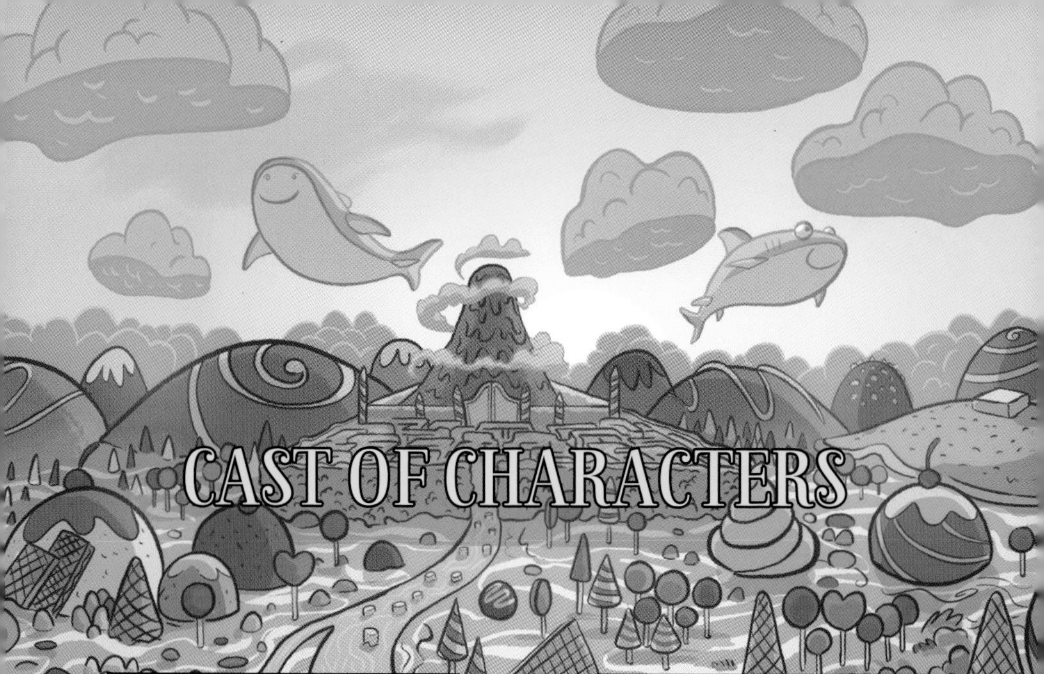

CAST OF CHARACTERS

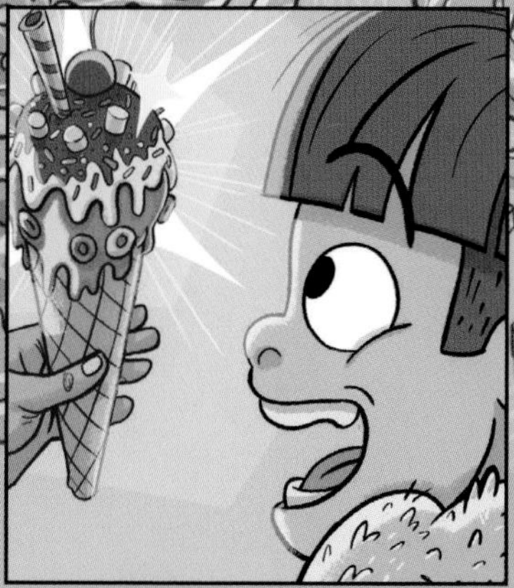

Michael is a boy with a taste for candy and adventure.

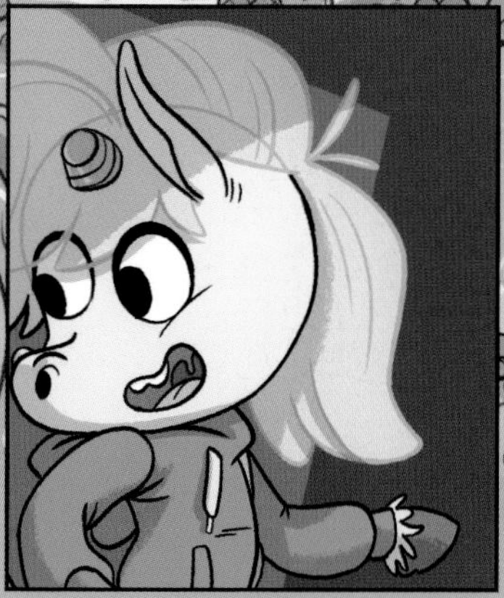

The **Unicorn** has lost his horn in Sweetlandia. He needs help getting it back.

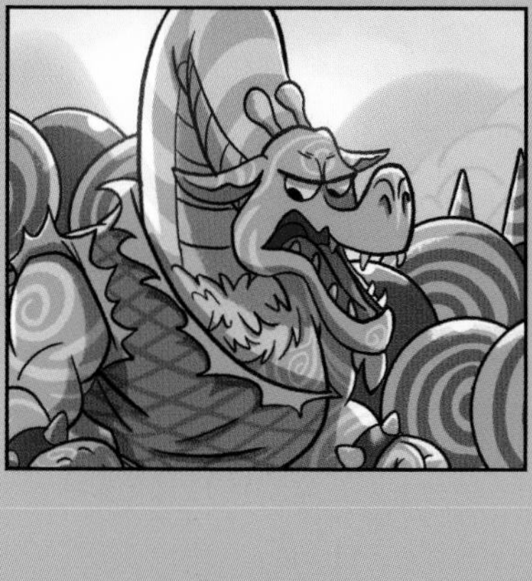

The **Taffee Giraffee** is the Guardian of the Gingerbread Gate.

HOW TO READ A GRAPHIC NOVEL

Graphic novels are easy to read. Boxes called panels show you how to follow the story. Look at the panels from left to right and top to bottom.

Read the word boxes and word balloons from left to right as well. Don't forget the sound and action words in the pictures.

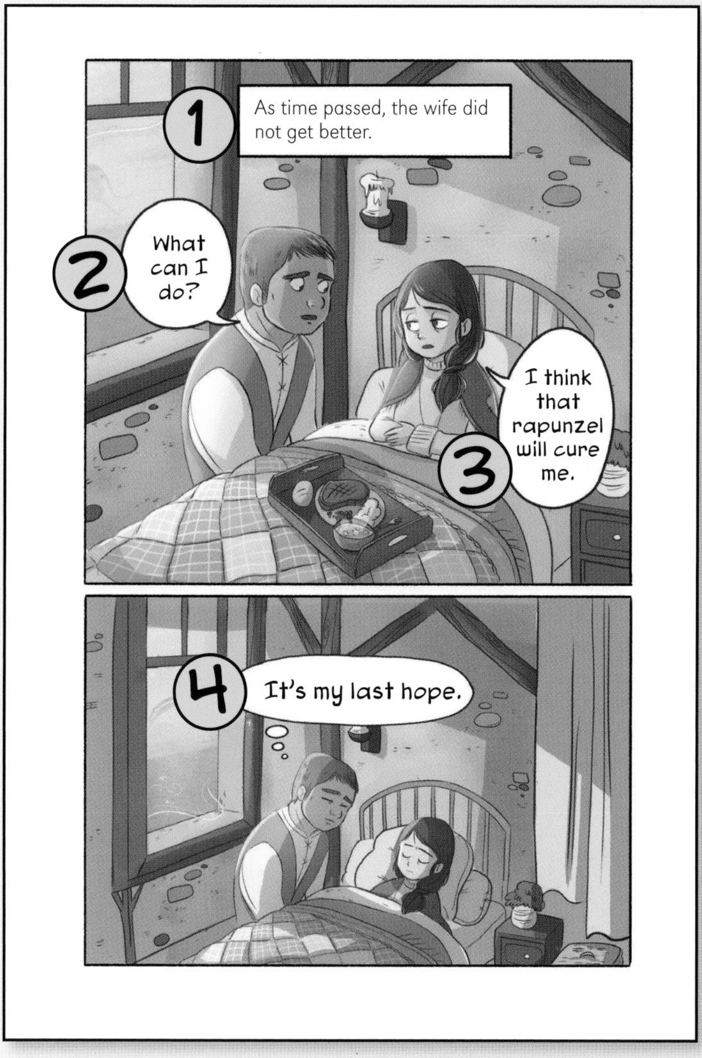
1
As time passed, the wife did not get better.
2
What can I do?
3
I think that rapunzel will cure me.
4
It's my last hope.

The pictures and the words work together to tell the whole story.

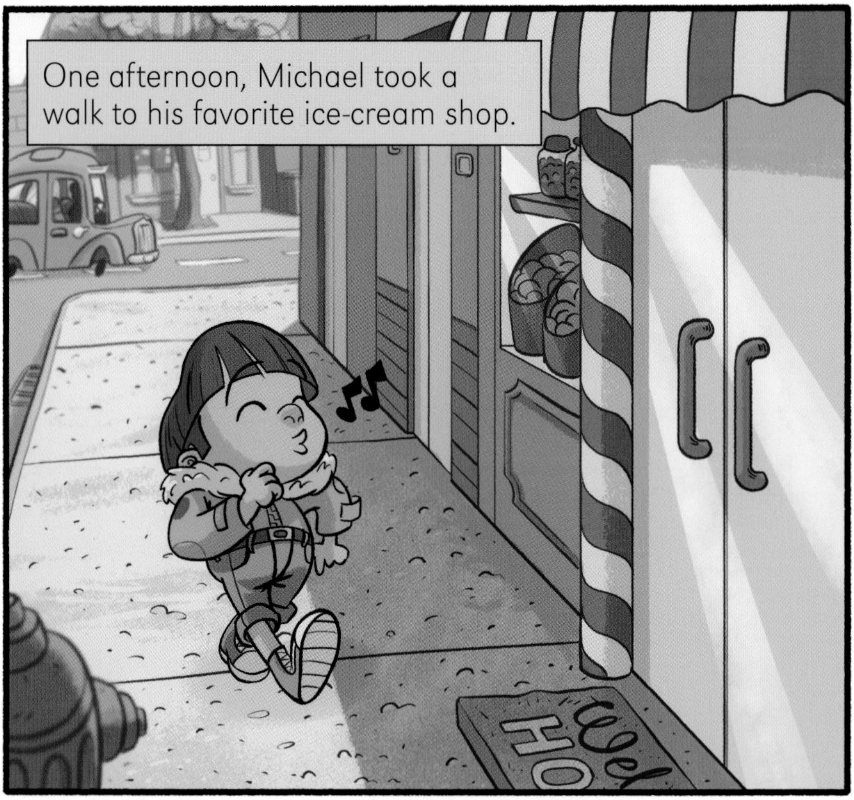
One afternoon, Michael took a walk to his favorite ice-cream shop.

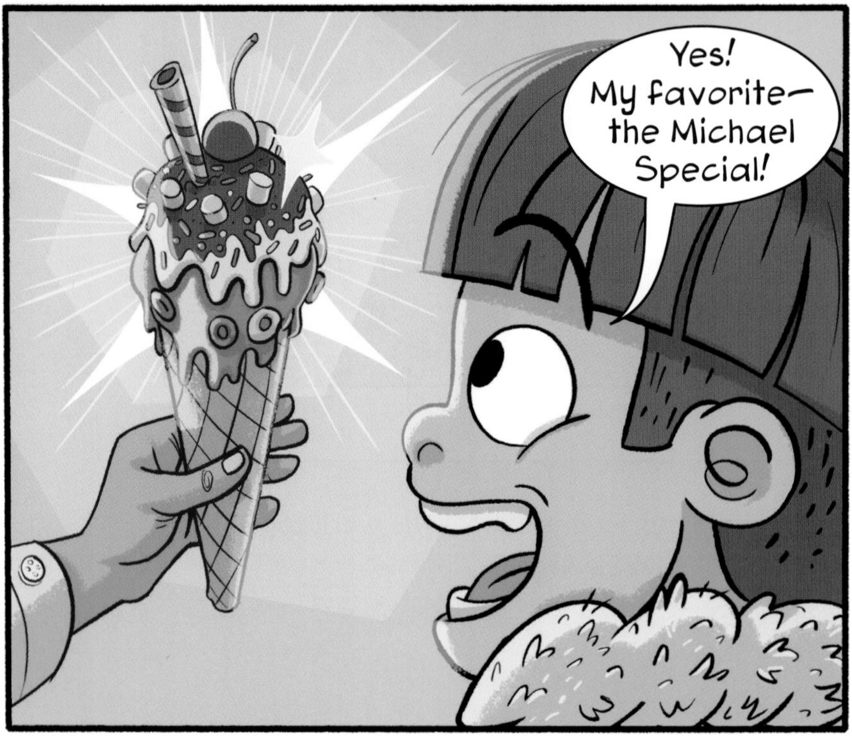
Yes! My favorite—the Michael Special!

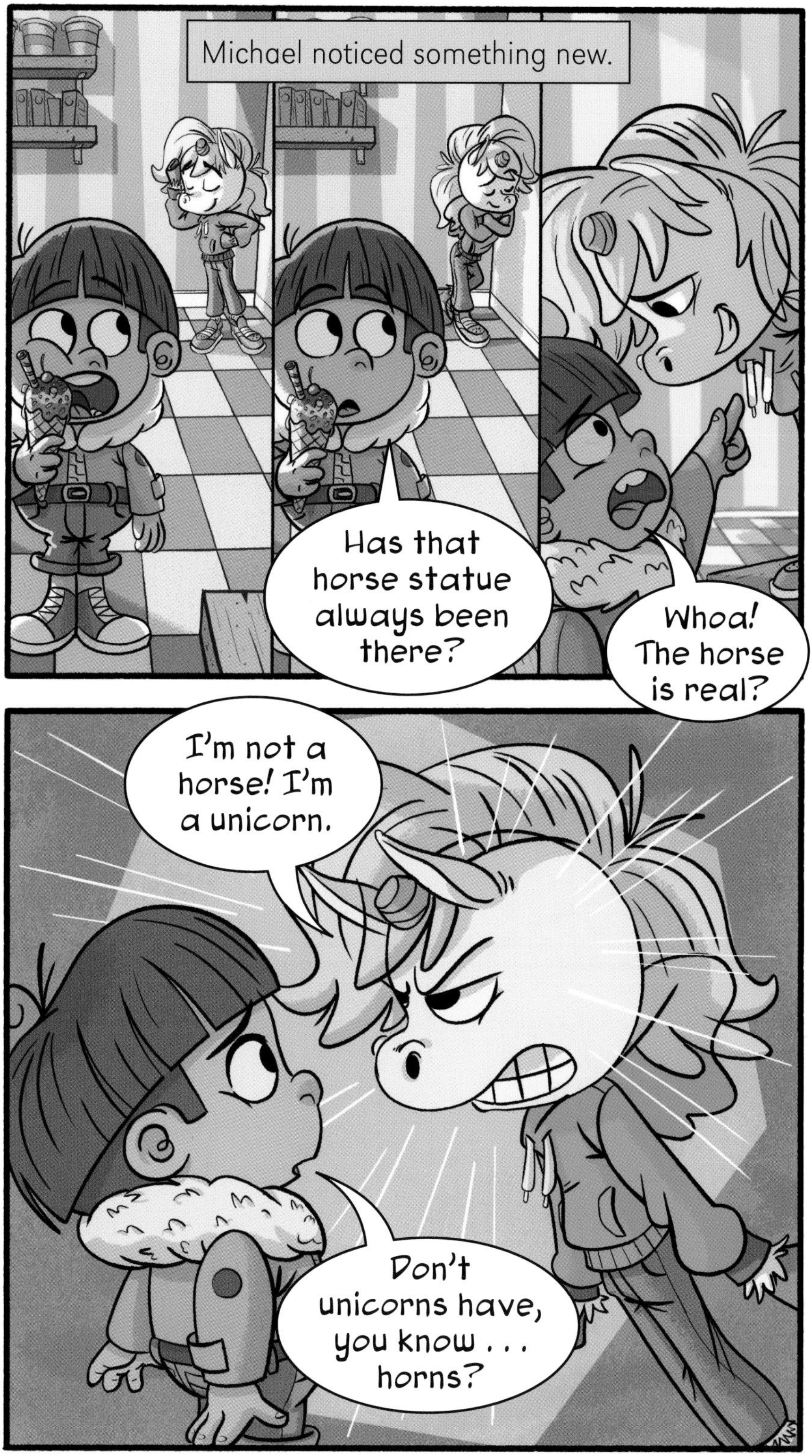
Michael noticed something new.
Has that horse statue always been there?
Whoa! The horse is real?
I'm not a horse! I'm a unicorn.
Don't unicorns have, you know . . . horns?

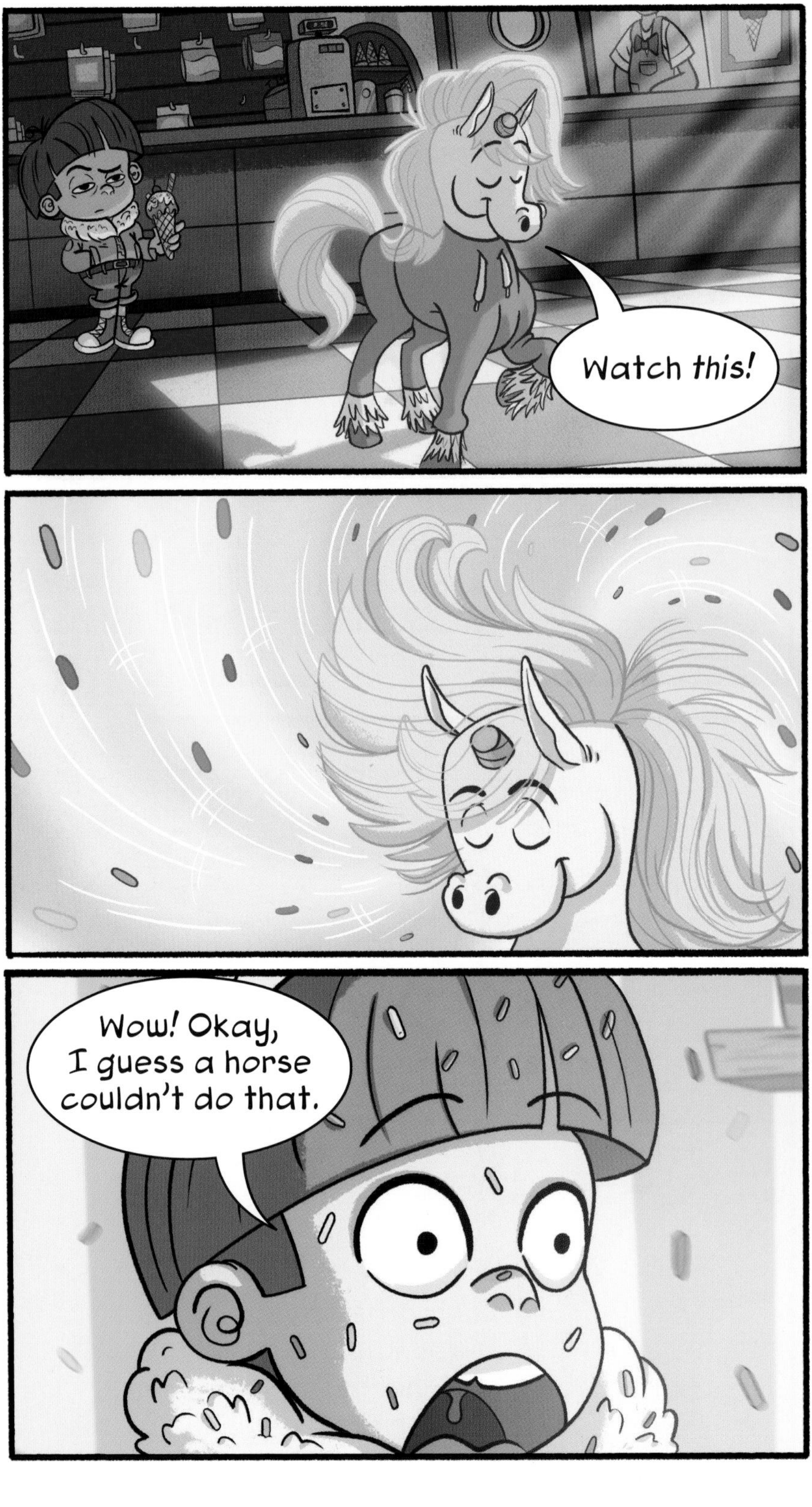
Watch this!
Wow! Okay, I guess a horse couldn't do that.

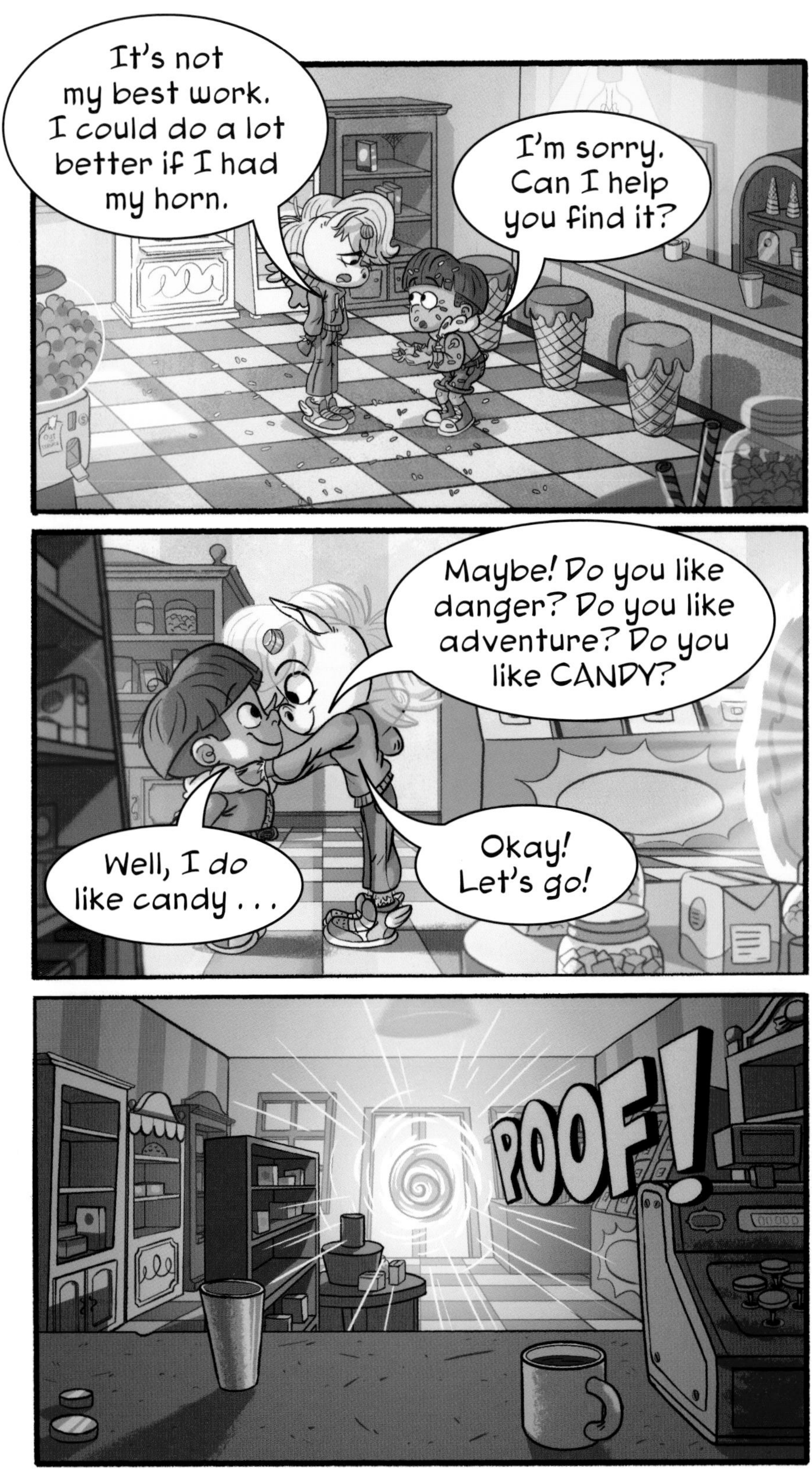
It's not my best work. I could do a lot better if I had my horn.
I'm sorry. Can I help you find it?
Maybe! Do you like danger? Do you like adventure? Do you like CANDY?
Well, I do like candy . . .
Okay! Let's go!
POOF!

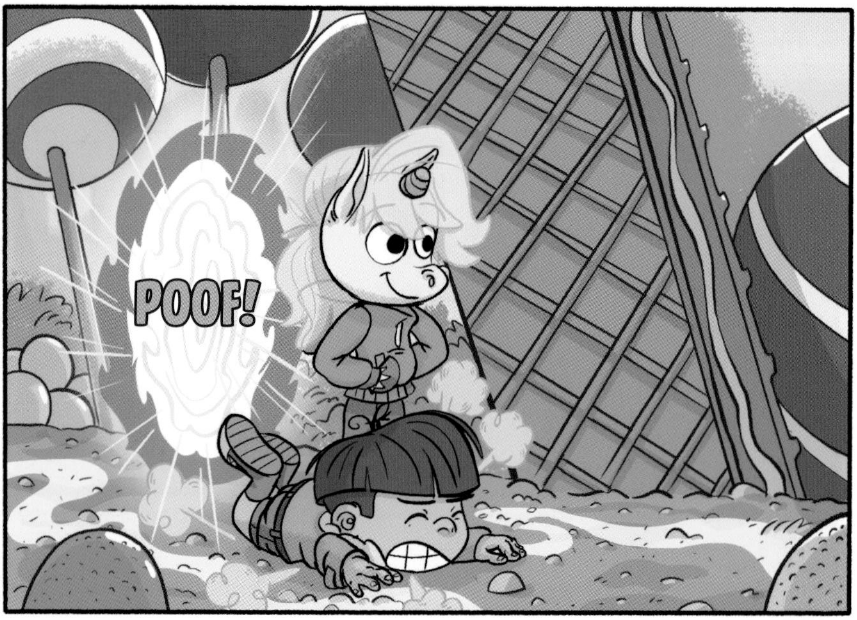
POOF!

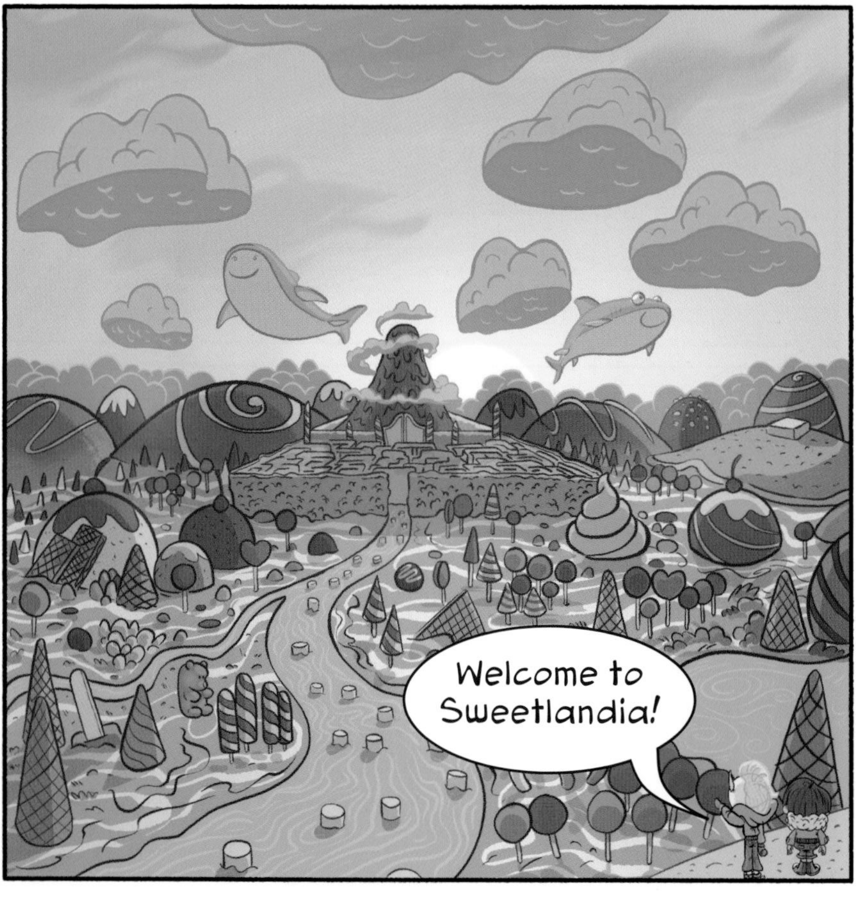
Welcome to Sweetlandia!

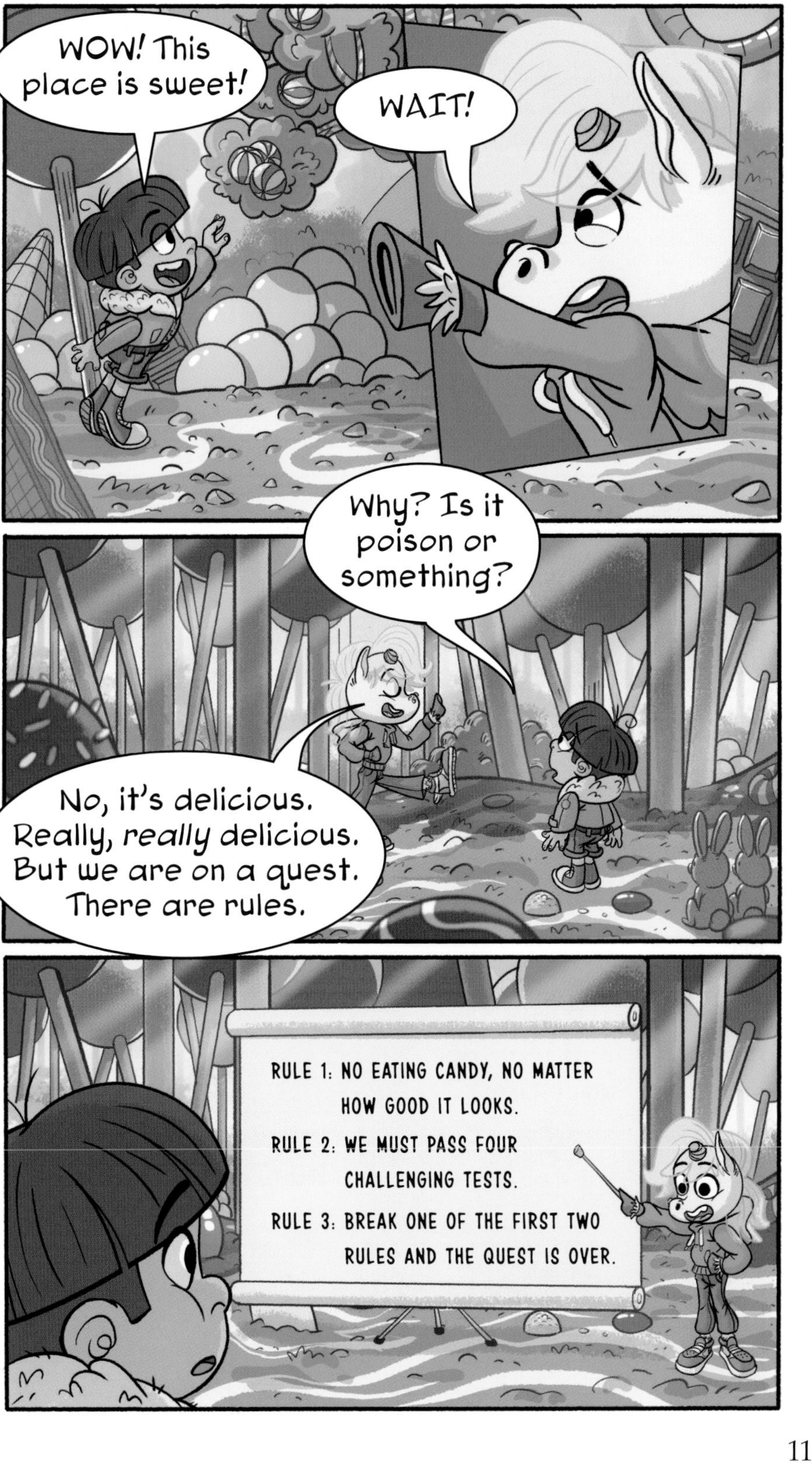
WOW! This place is sweet!
WAIT!
Why? Is it poison or something?
No, it's delicious. Really, *really* delicious. But we are on a quest. There are rules.
RULE 1: NO EATING CANDY, NO MATTER HOW GOOD IT LOOKS.
RULE 2: WE MUST PASS FOUR CHALLENGING TESTS.
RULE 3: BREAK ONE OF THE FIRST TWO RULES AND THE QUEST IS OVER.

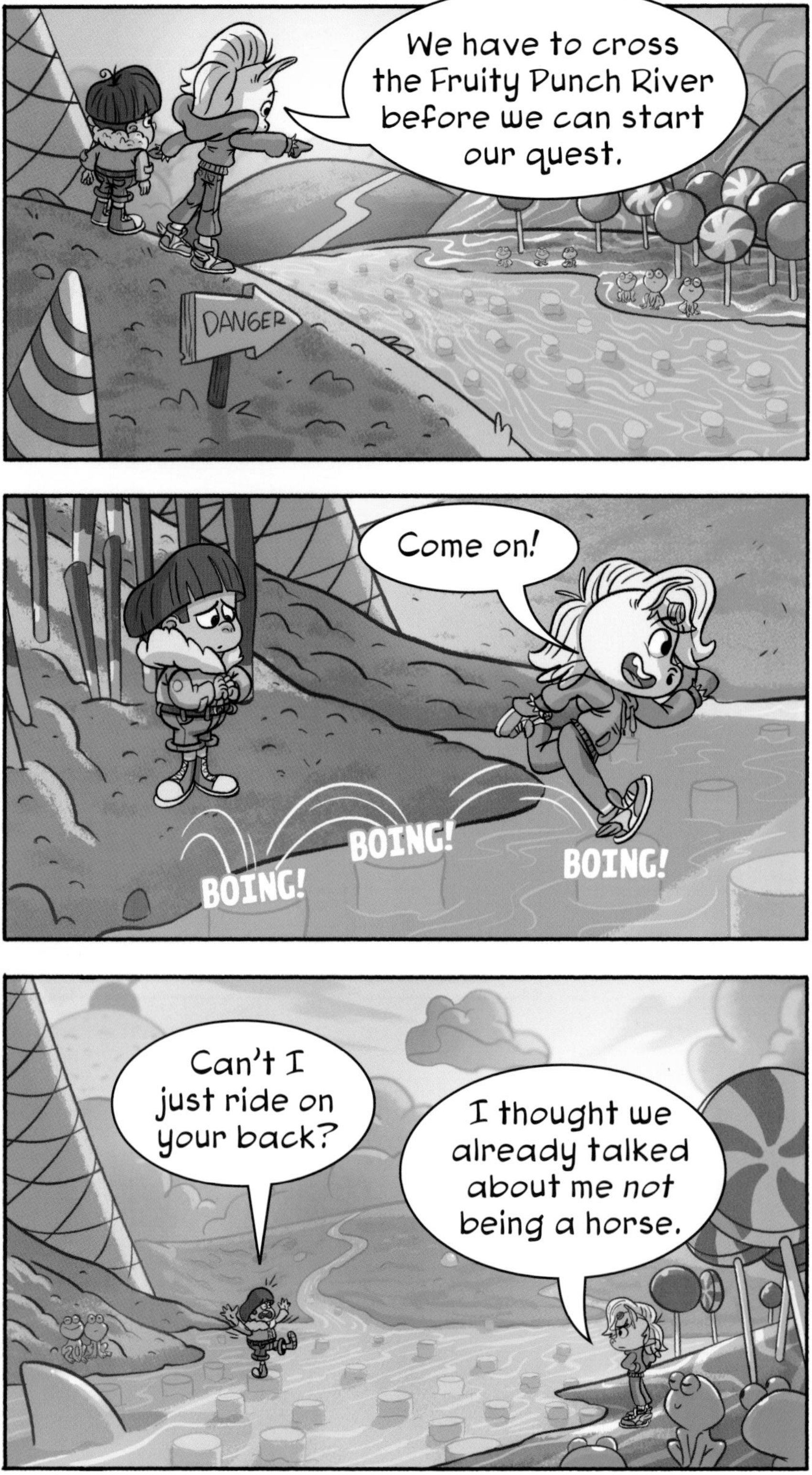
We have to cross the Fruity Punch River before we can start our quest.
DANGER
Come on!
BOING!
BOING!
BOING!
Can't I just ride on your back?
I thought we already talked about me *not* being a horse.

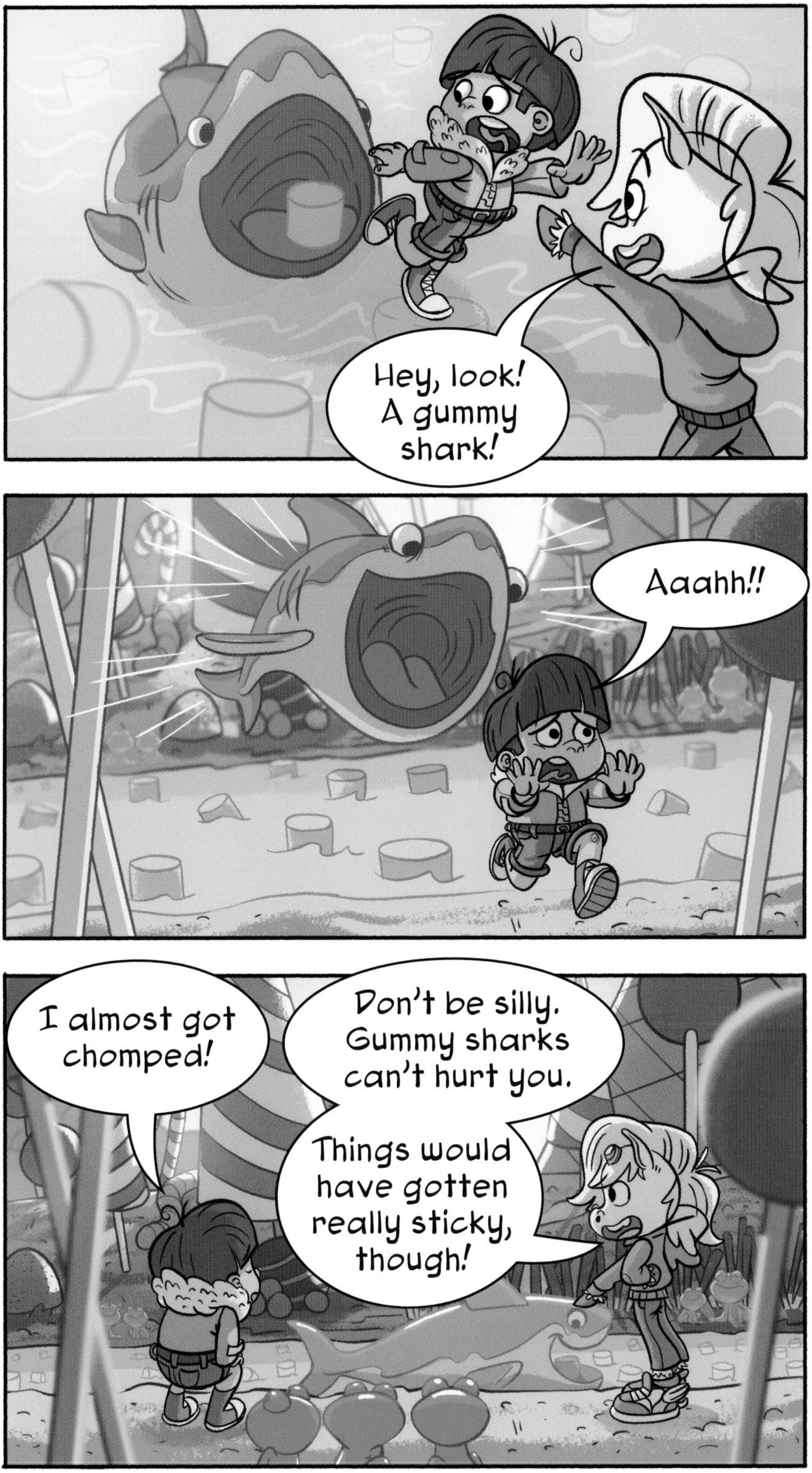
Hey, look! A gummy shark!
Aaahh!!
I almost got chomped!
Don't be silly. Gummy sharks can't hurt you.
Things would have gotten really sticky, though!

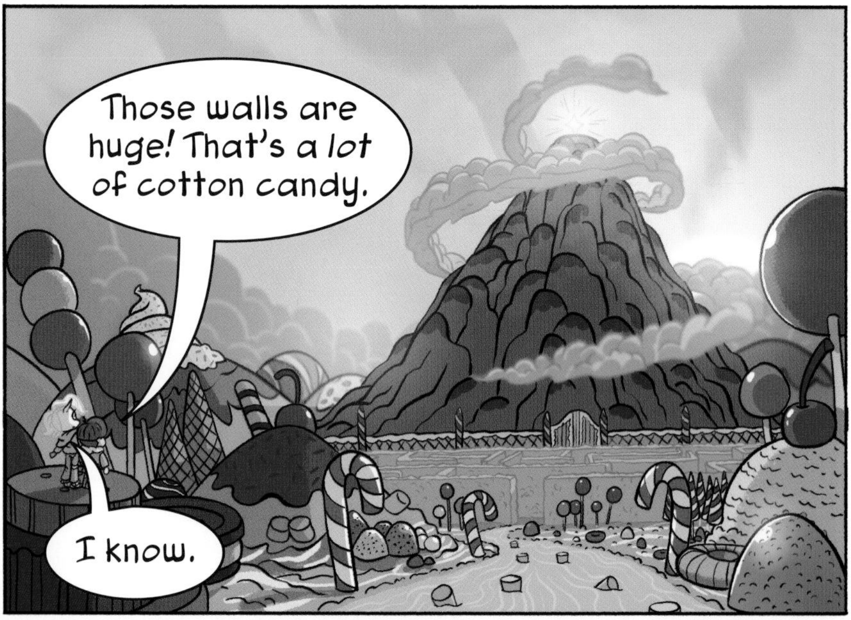
Those walls are huge! That's a *lot* of cotton candy.
I know.

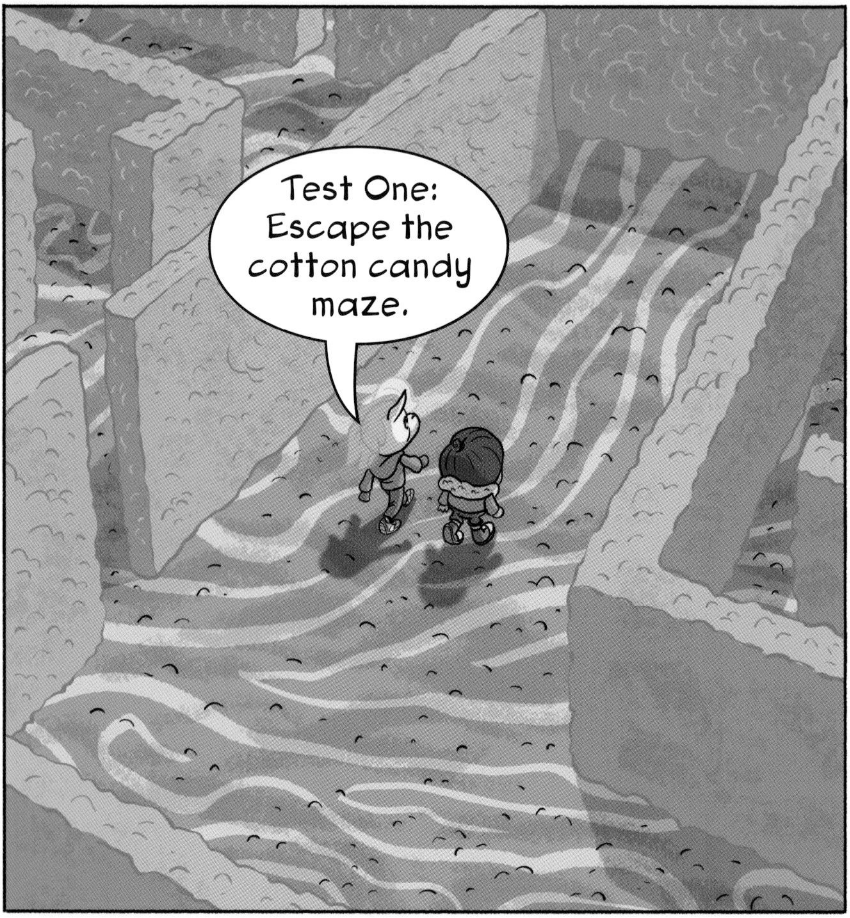
Test One: Escape the cotton candy maze.

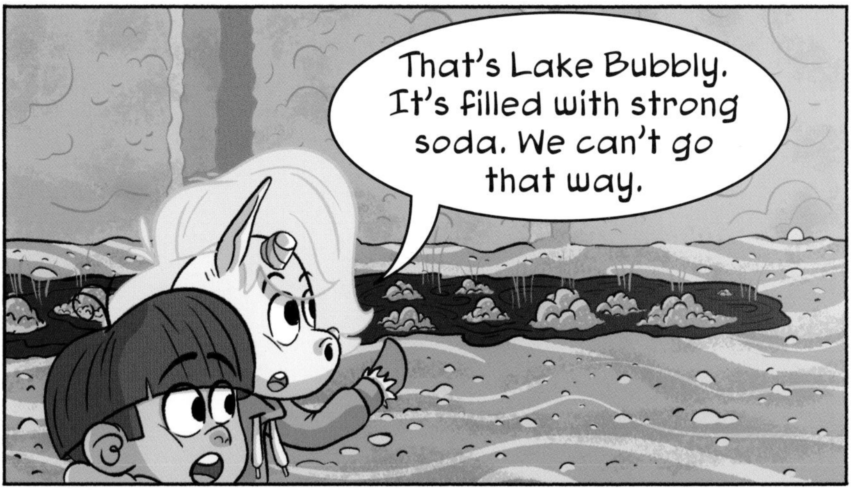
That's Lake Bubbly. It's filled with strong soda. We can't go that way.

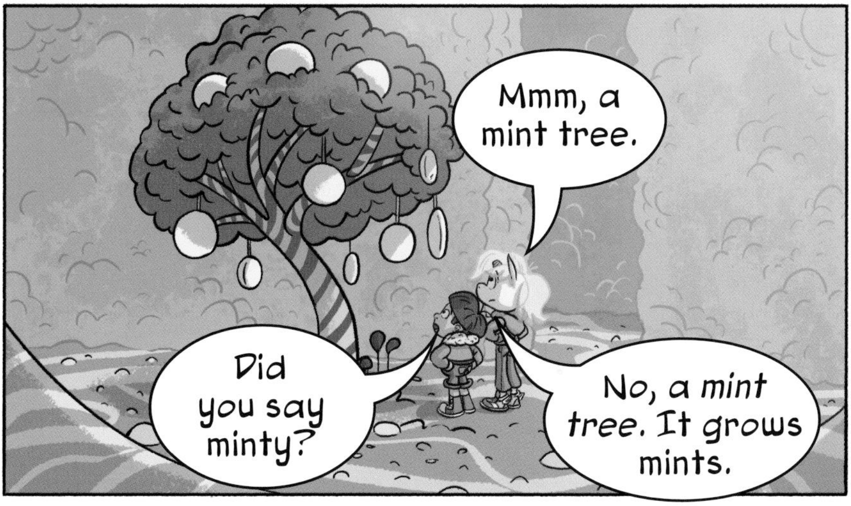
Mmm, a mint tree.
Did you say minty?
No, a *mint tree*. It grows mints.

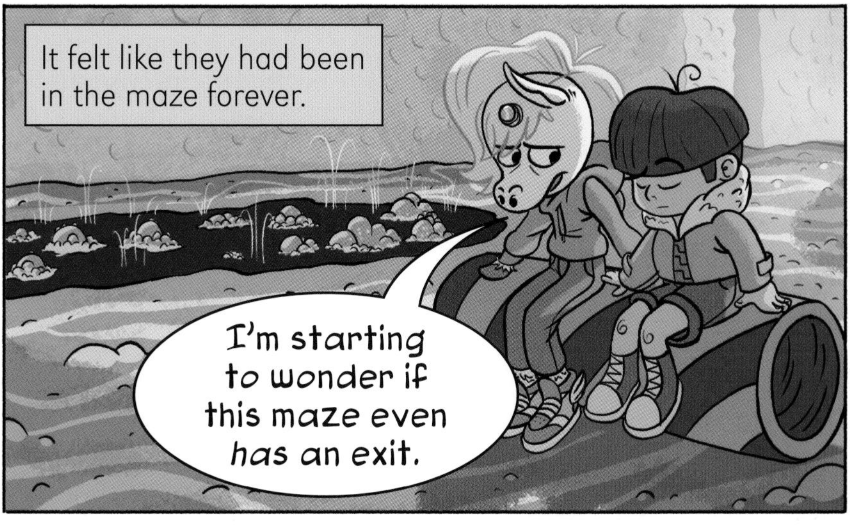
It felt like they had been in the maze forever.
I'm starting to wonder if this maze even *has* an exit.

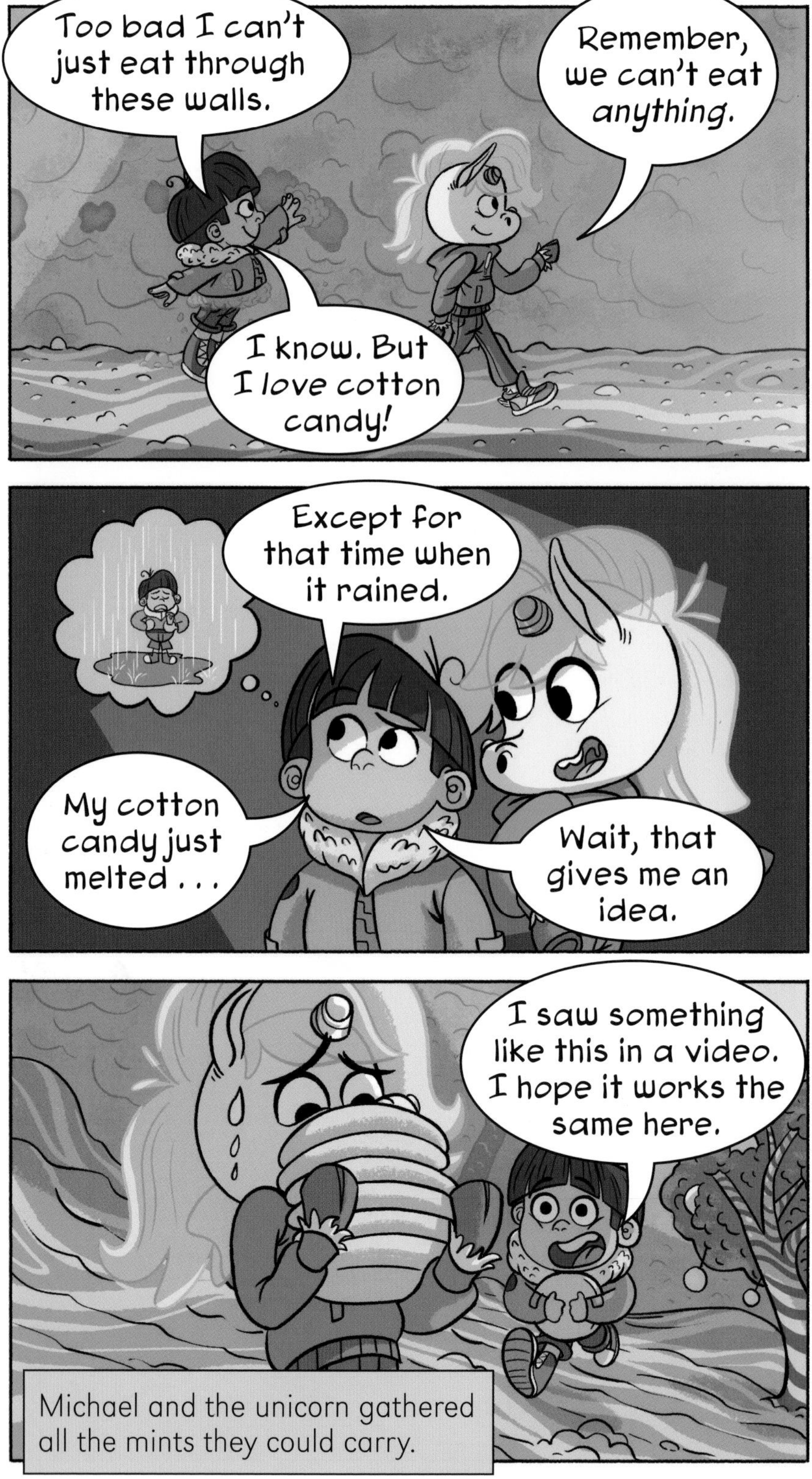
Too bad I can't just eat through these walls.
Remember, we can't eat *anything*.
I know. But I *love* cotton candy!
Except for that time when it rained.
My cotton candy just melted . . .
Wait, that gives me an idea.
I saw something like this in a video. I hope it works the same here.
Michael and the unicorn gathered all the mints they could carry.

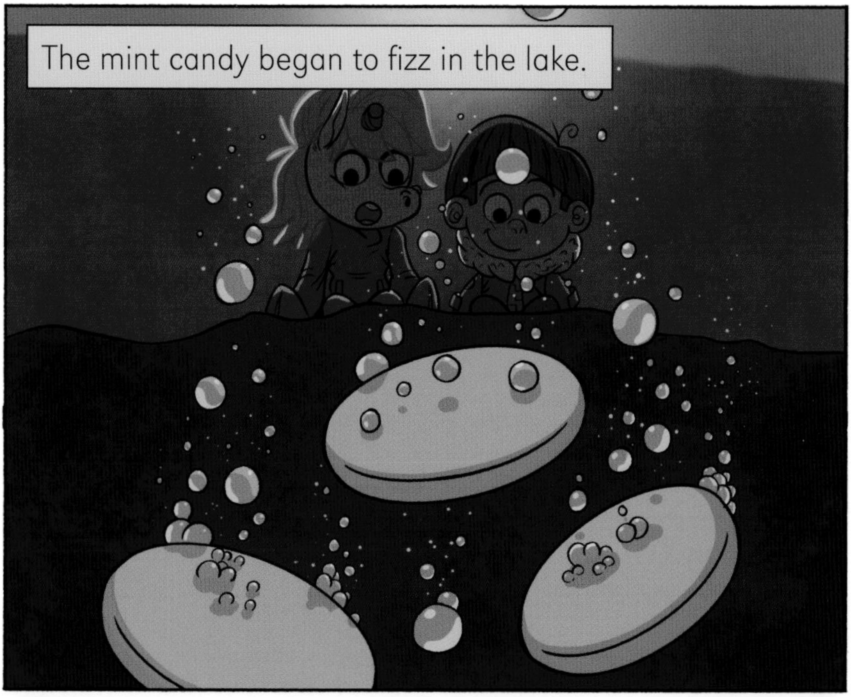
The mint candy began to fizz in the lake.

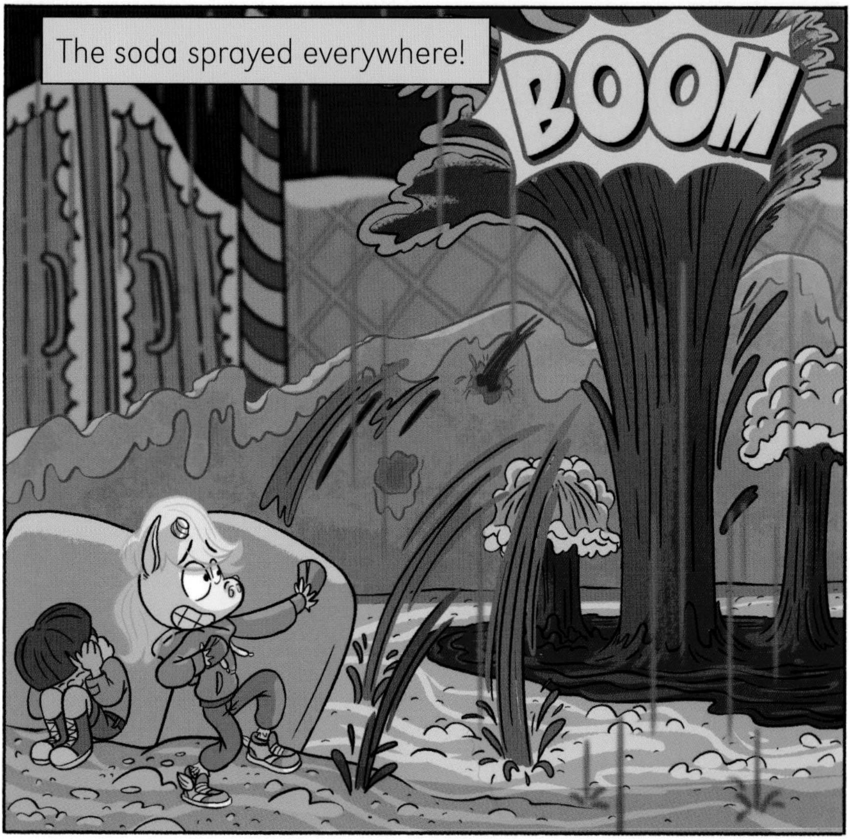
The soda sprayed everywhere!
BOOM

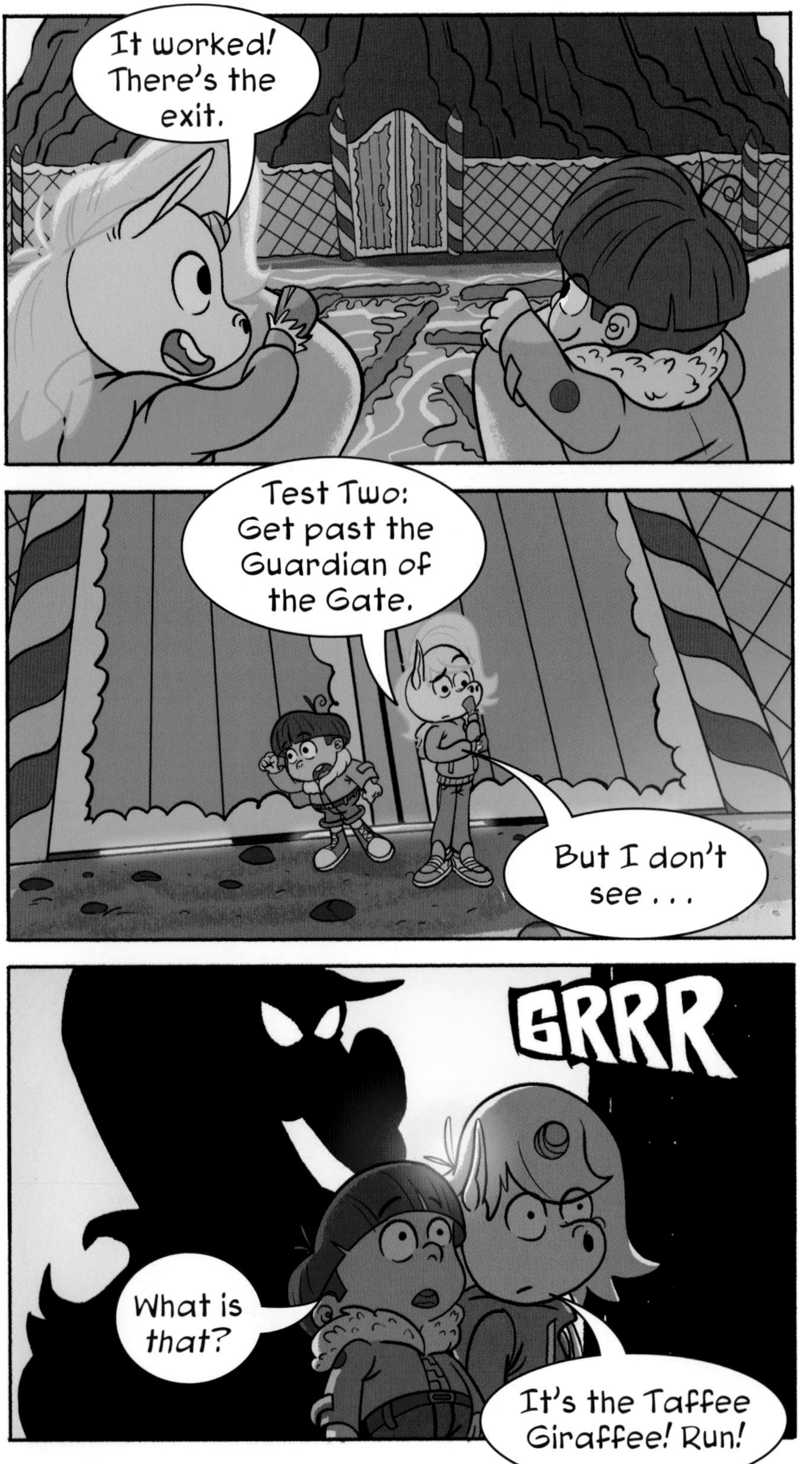
It worked! There's the exit.
Test Two: Get past the Guardian of the Gate.
But I don't see . . .
GRRR
What is that?
It's the Taffee Giraffee! Run!

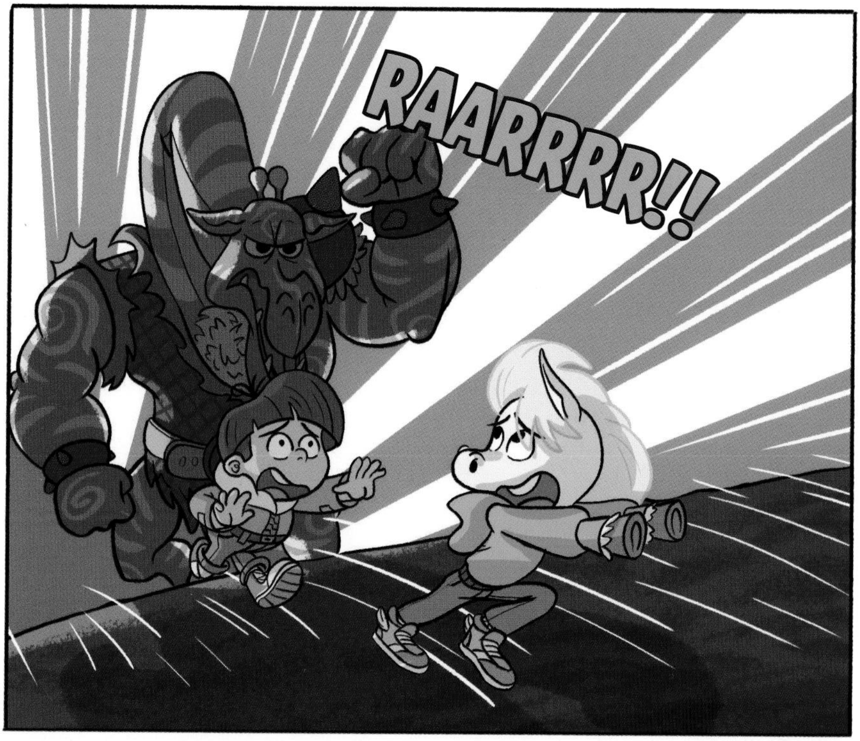
RAARRRRR!!

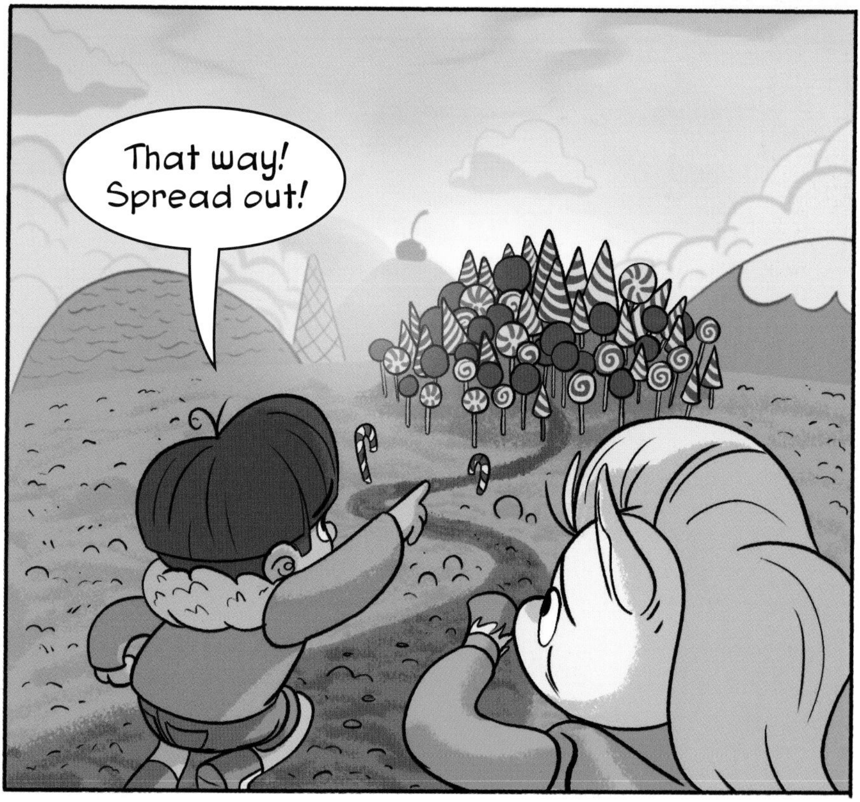
That way!
Spread out!

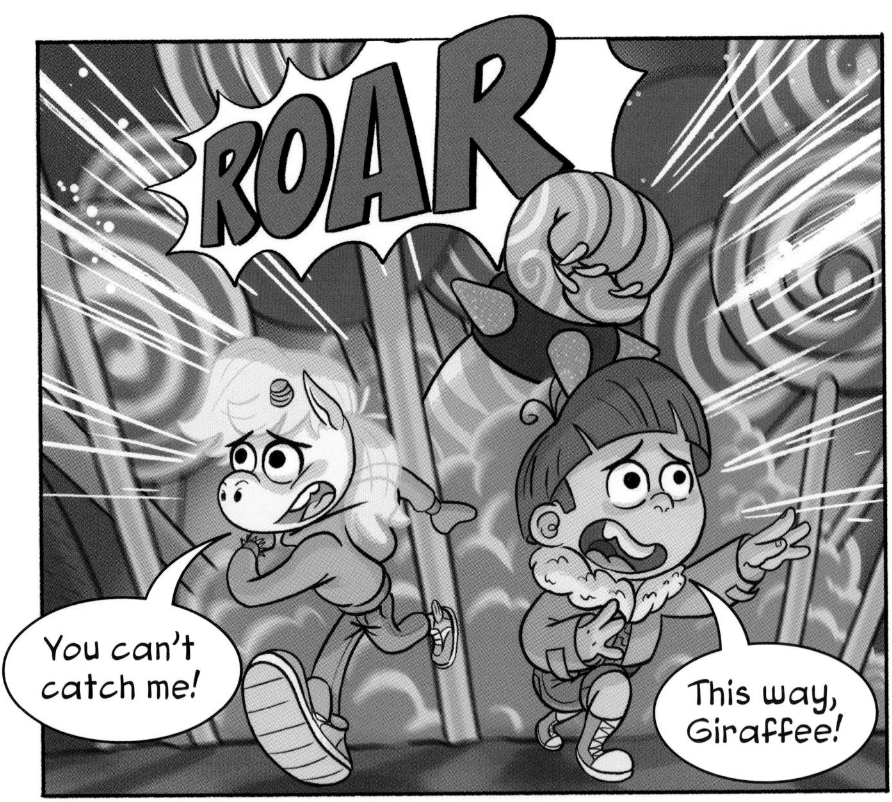
ROAR
You can't catch me!
This way, Giraffee!

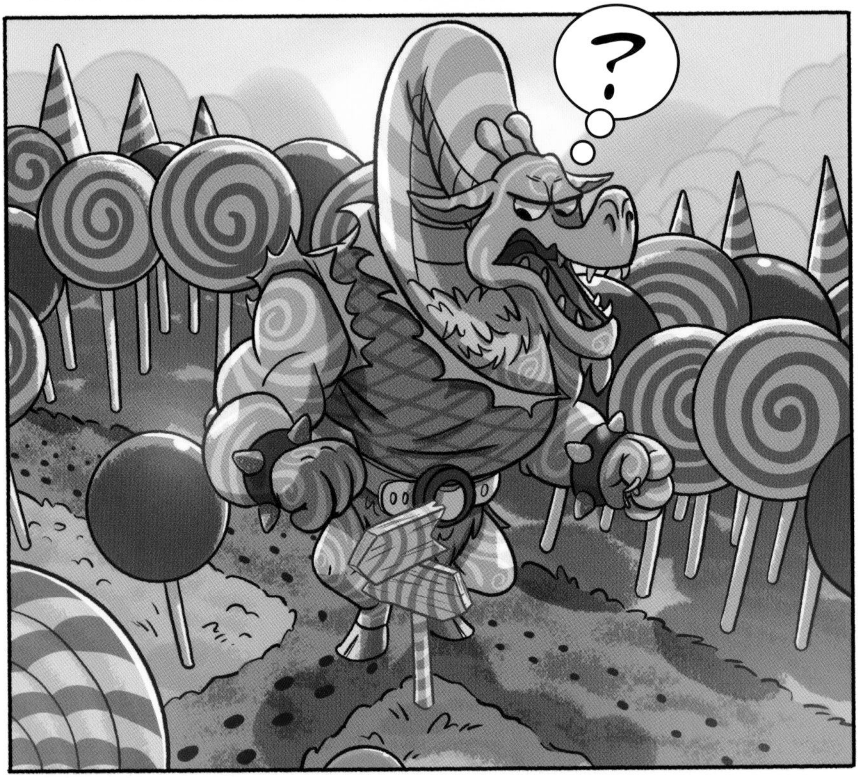
?

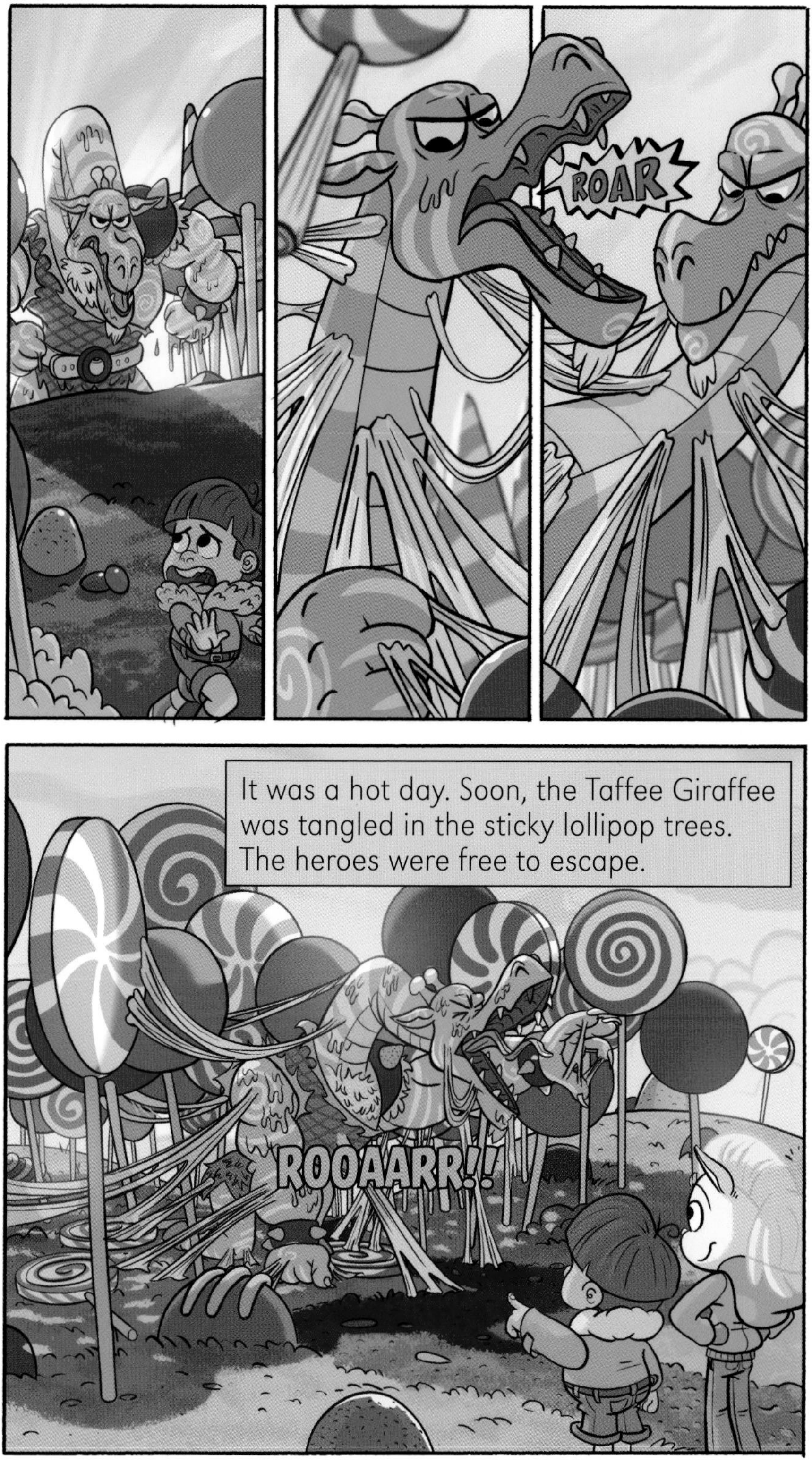
ROAR
It was a hot day. Soon, the Taffee Giraffee was tangled in the sticky lollipop trees. The heroes were free to escape.
ROOAARR!!

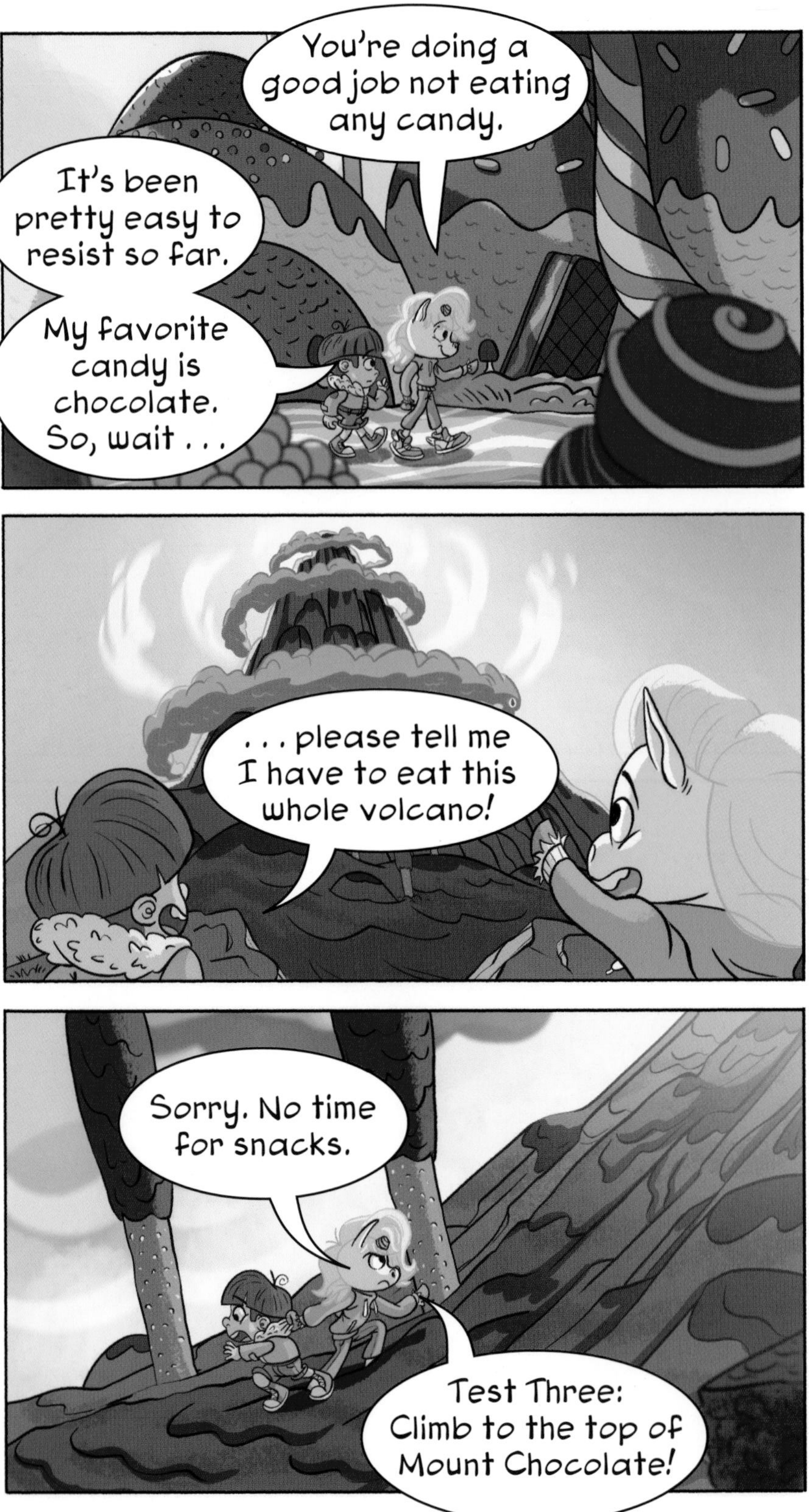
You're doing a good job not eating any candy.
It's been pretty easy to resist so far.
My favorite candy is chocolate. So, wait . . .
. . . please tell me I have to eat this whole volcano!
Sorry. No time for snacks.
Test Three: Climb to the top of Mount Chocolate!

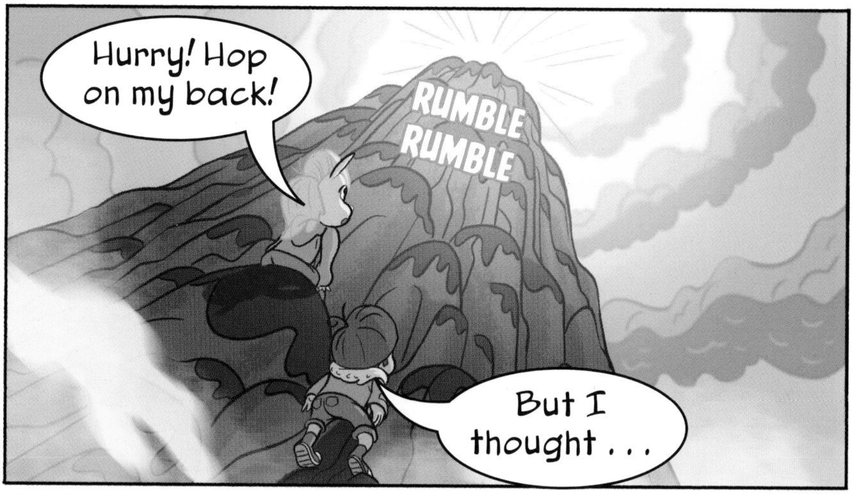
Hurry! Hop on my back!
RUMBLE RUMBLE
But I thought . . .

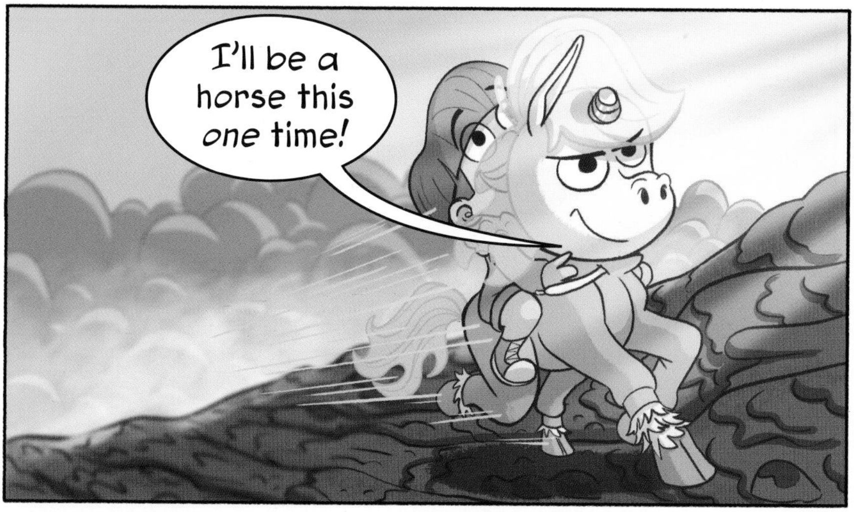
I'll be a horse this *one* time!

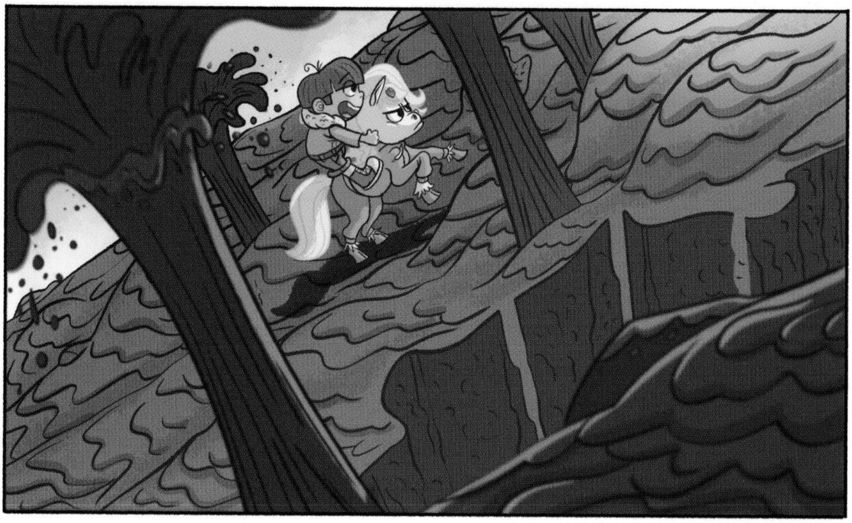

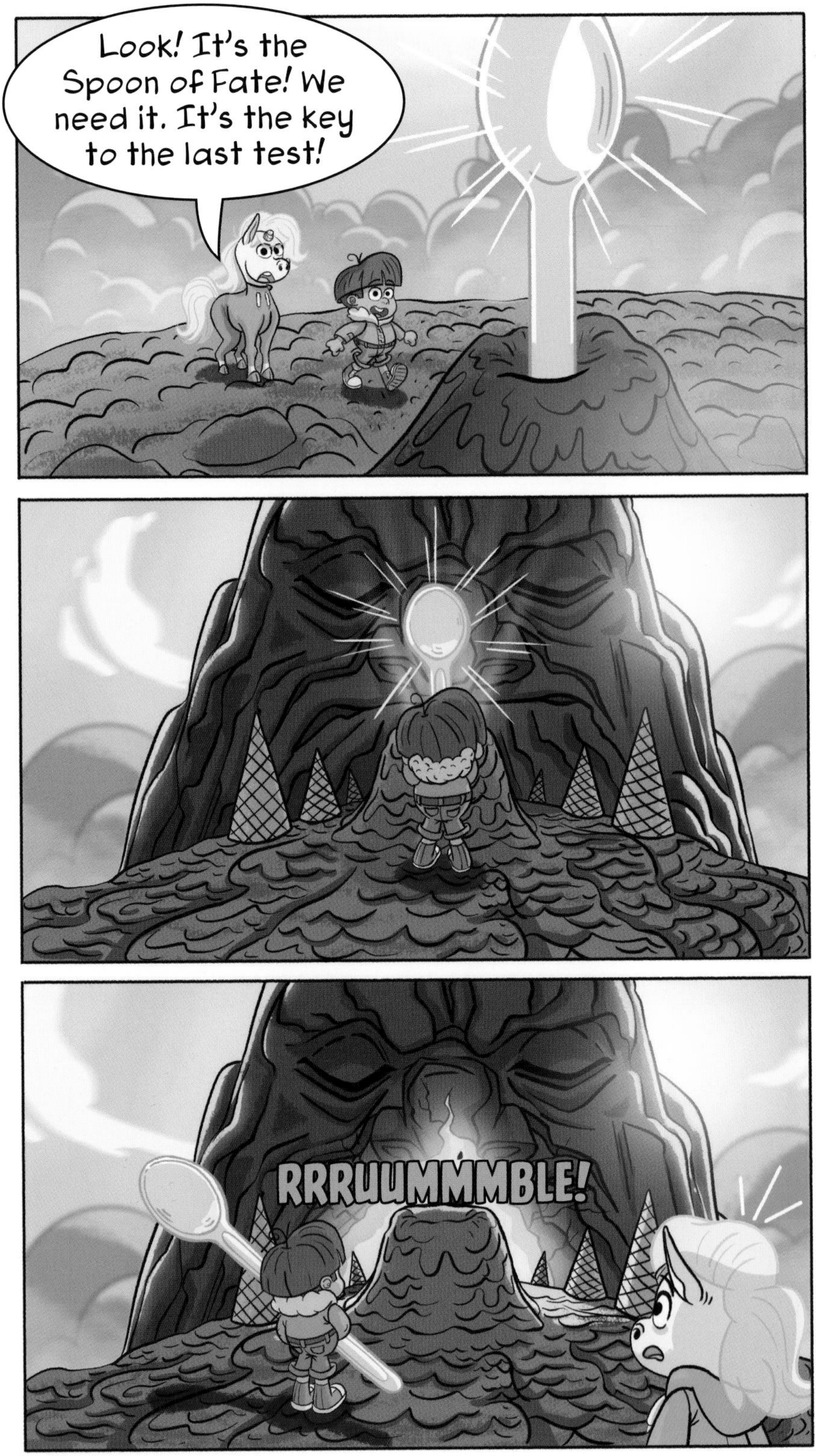
Look! It's the Spoon of Fate! We need it. It's the key to the last test!
RRRUUMMMBLE!

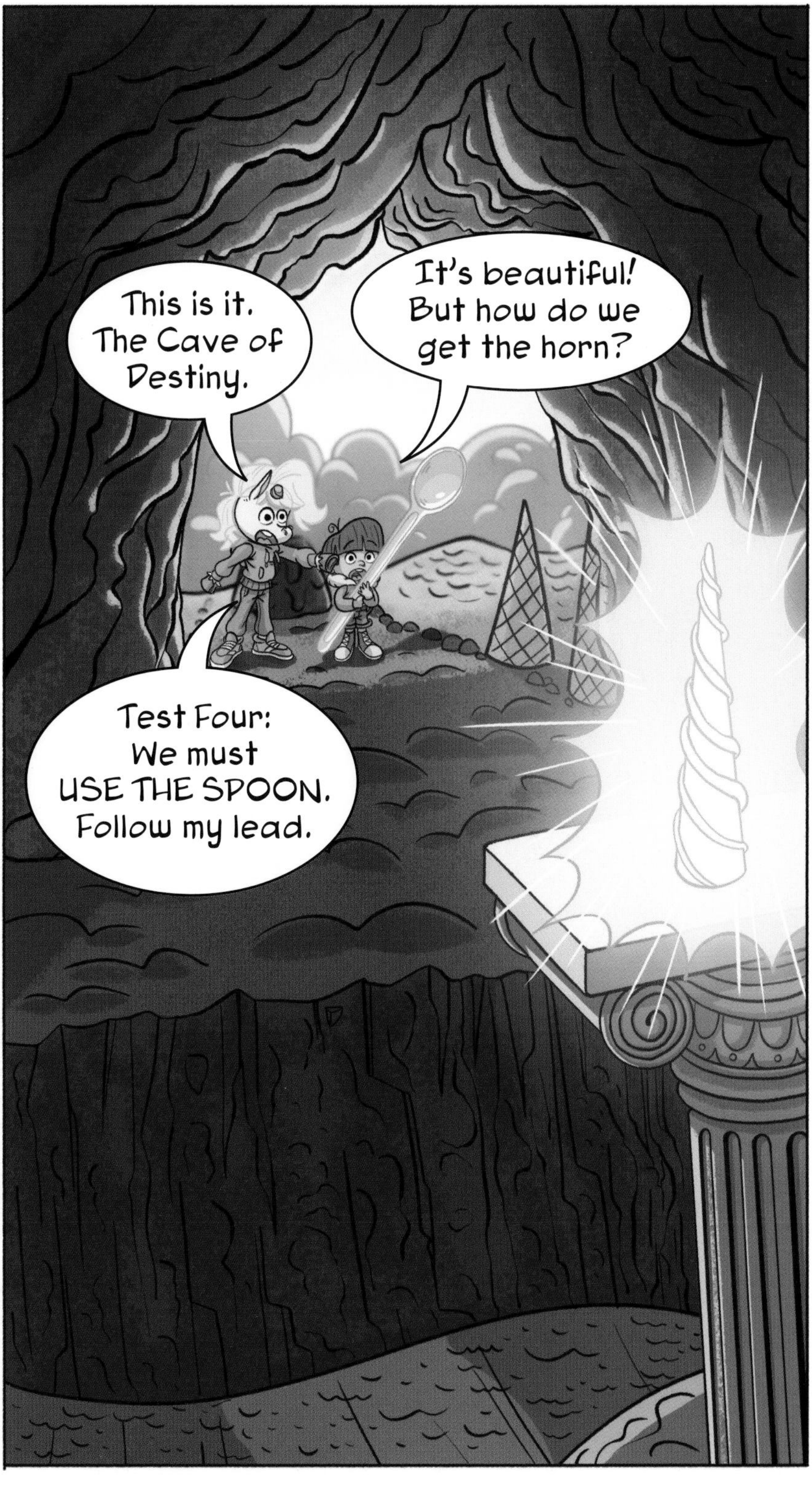
This is it. The Cave of Destiny.
It's beautiful! But how do we get the horn?
Test Four: We must USE THE SPOON. Follow my lead.

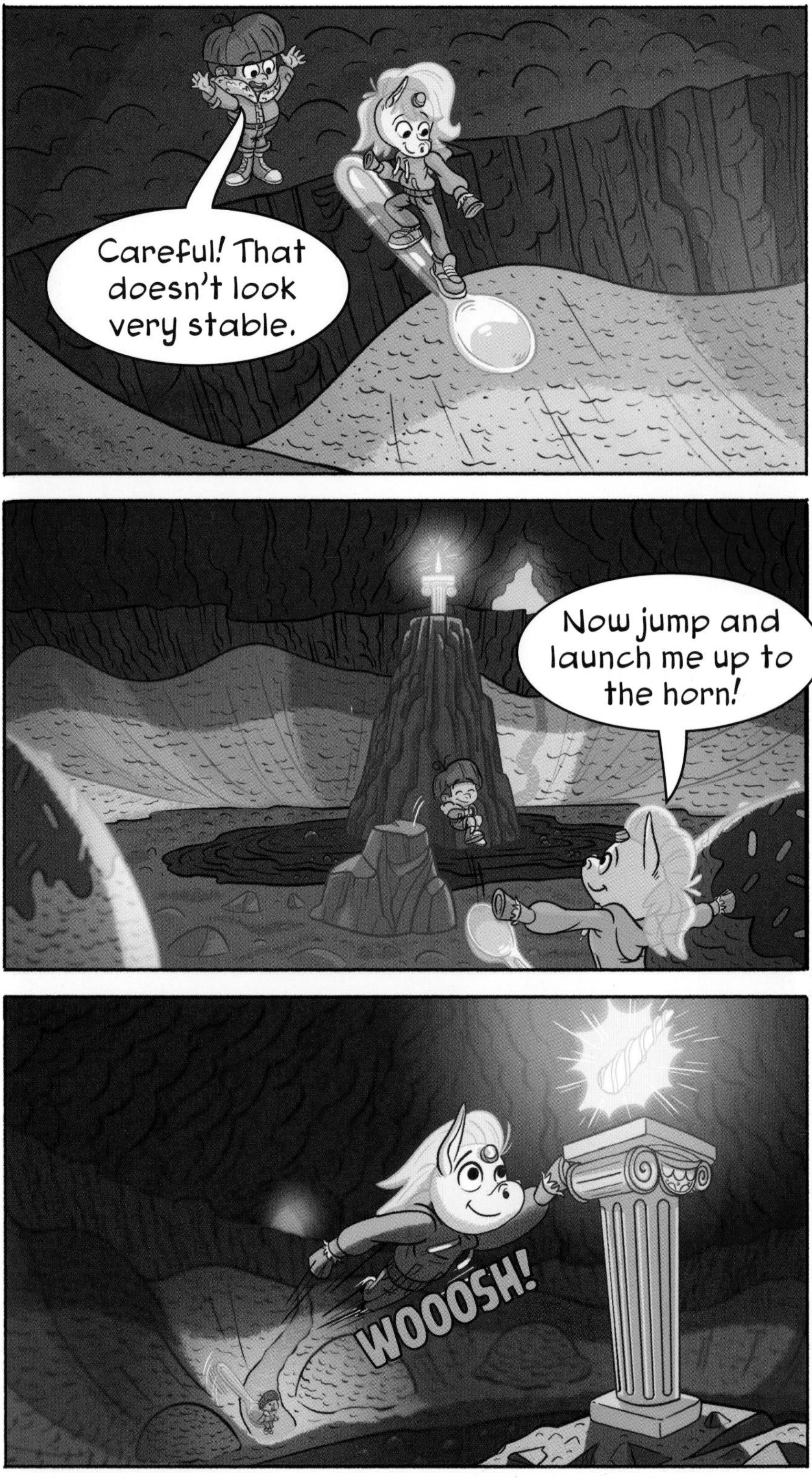
Careful! That doesn't look very stable.
Now jump and launch me up to the horn!
WOOOSH!

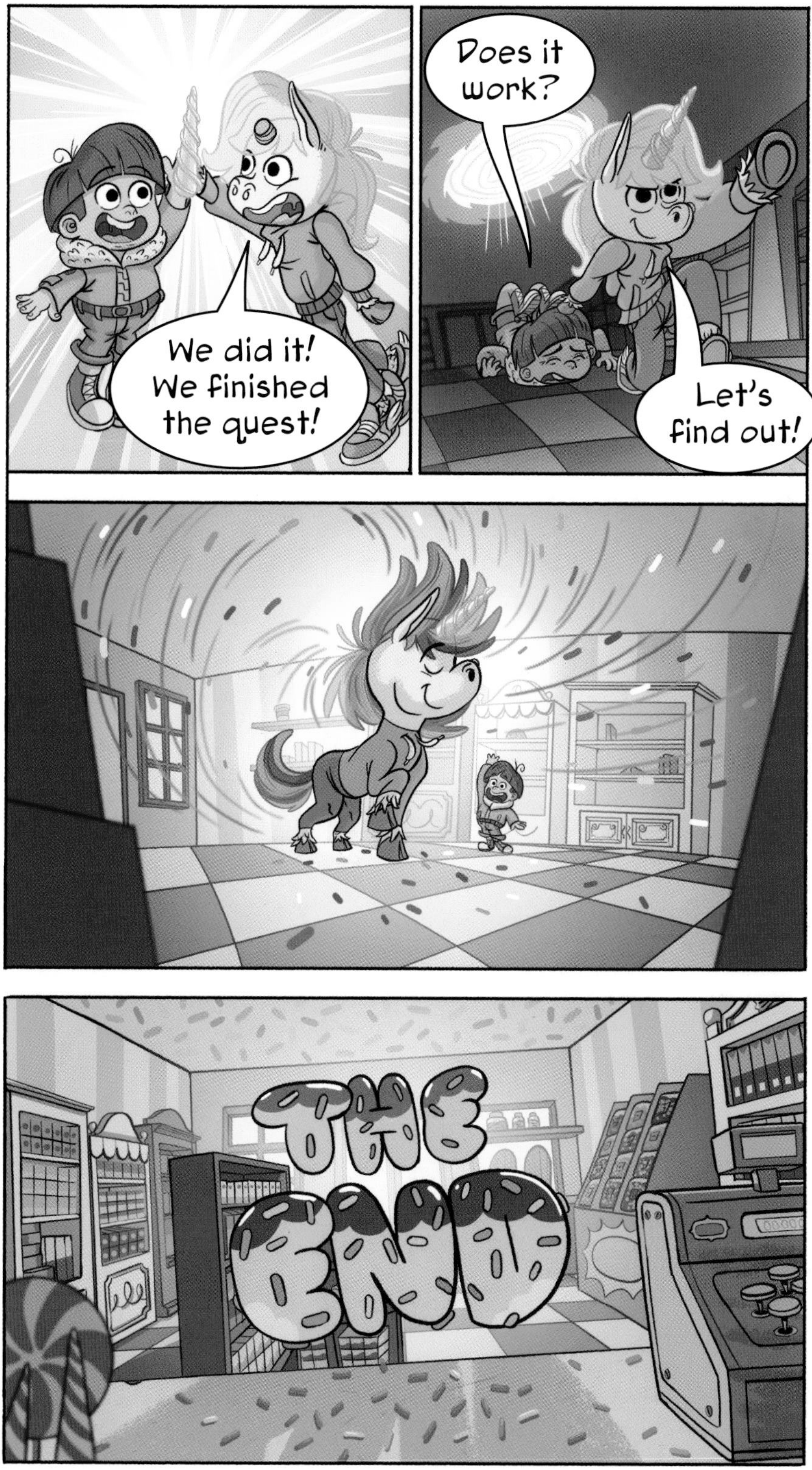
We did it! We finished the quest!
Does it work?
Let's find out!
THE END

WRITING PROMPTS

1. Sweetlandia probably smells pretty good! What smells do you love? Write a description of one. Imagine it will be read by someone who has never experienced that smell before.

2. Draw a picture of Sweetlandia. What kind of candies would be in your fantasy land? Add a description or a list of those sweets.

3. Flip back through the story. How can you tell that Michael likes candy? Choose one or two pictures and write a short explanation of what is happening in them.

DISCUSSION QUESTIONS

1. Have you ever had to help a friend find something they lost?

2. Out of all the tests Michael had to go through, which would be the hardest one for you to pass?

3. Imagine you are in a candy land. Think of other candy-themed quests you might have to do.

SWEETLANDIA ROCK CANDY

What You Need:

- quart-size glass jar with wide mouth
- ruler
- scissors
- thick cotton thread
- pencil
- 4 cups (800 grams) white sugar
- 2 cups (473 milliliters) water
- medium-size pot
- ½ to 1 teaspoon (2.5 to 5 ml) flavoring extract or oil (optional)
- 2 drops food coloring (optional)
- paper towels

What You Do:

Step 1: Clean the glass jar with hot water.

Step 2: Measure and cut a piece of cotton thread the same height as the jar. Then tie the thread to the pencil.

Step 3: Set the pencil across the top of the jar. The thread should hang down inside the jar. Make sure the thread does not touch the bottom of the jar.

Step 4: Remove the pencil and thread from the jar. Dip the thread in water. Then roll it in white sugar. Set aside to dry.

Step 5: With an adult's help, pour the water into a pot. Then bring it to a boil over the stove. Add 1 cup of sugar. Stir well until it's dissolved. Repeat with the rest of the sugar, 1 cup at a time, until it is all added and dissolved. Remove the pot from the heat.

Step 6: Stir in the flavorings and food coloring, if desired. Then let the sugar syrup cool for 10 minutes.

Step 7: With the adult's help, pour the sugar syrup into the jar. Lower the thread into the jar and lay the pencil across the jar's top. Cover the top of the jar with a paper towel and set the jar in a cool place.

Step 8: Crystals should form in 2 to 4 hours. Let the rock candy grow until it is the size you want. Then remove and enjoy!

READ ALL THE AMAZING DISCOVER GRAPHICS BOOKS!

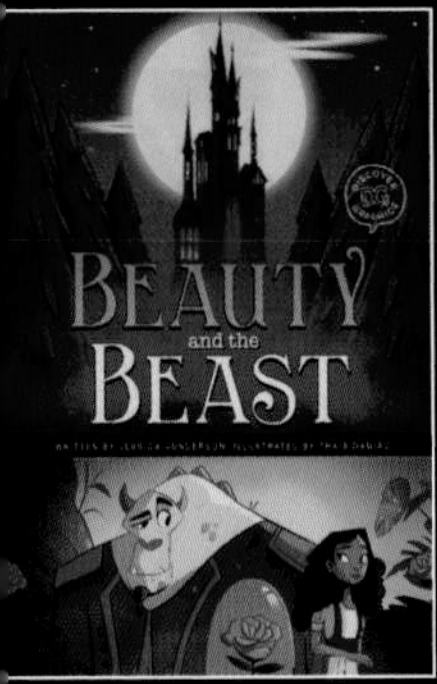
BEAUTY
and the
BEAST

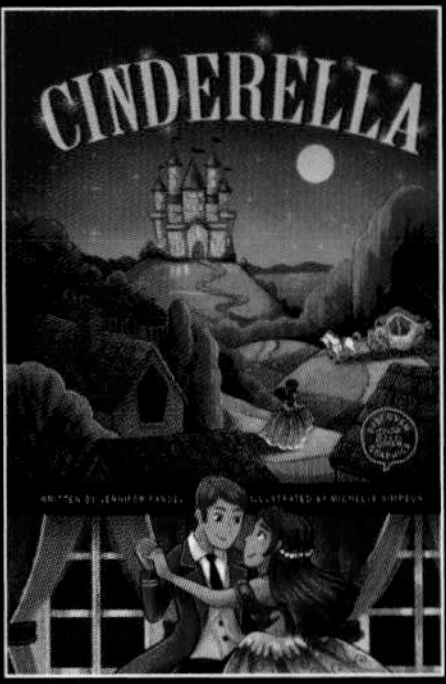
CINDERELLA

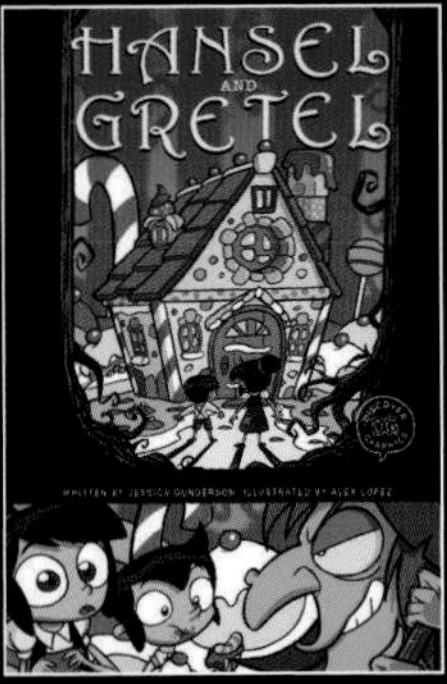
HANSEL
AND
GRETEL

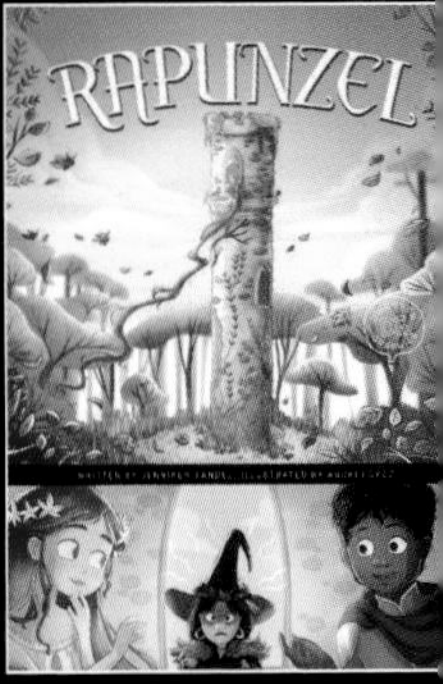
RAPUNZEL

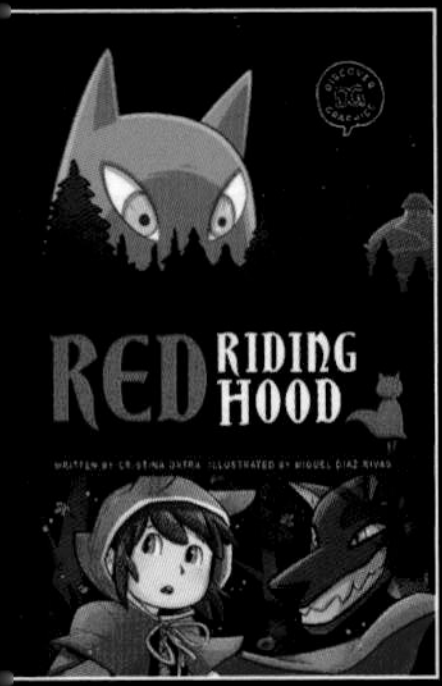
RED RIDING HOOD

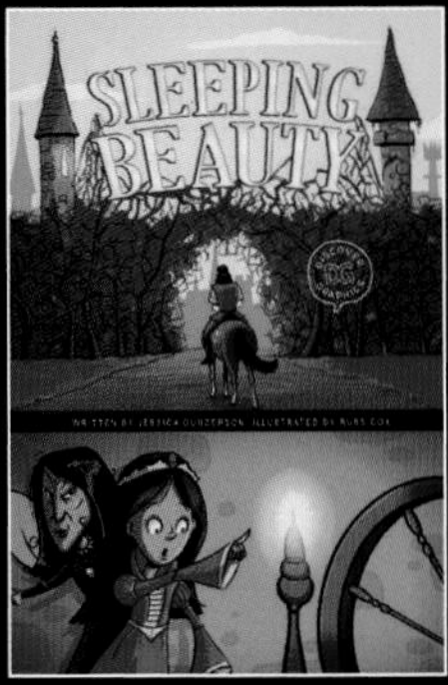
SLEEPING BEAUTY

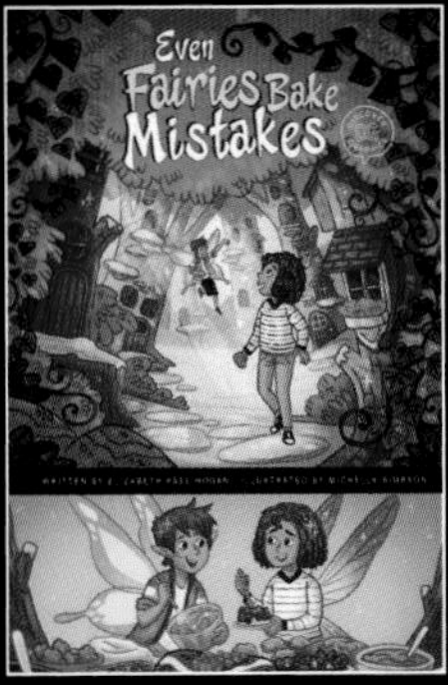
Even Fairies Bake Mistakes

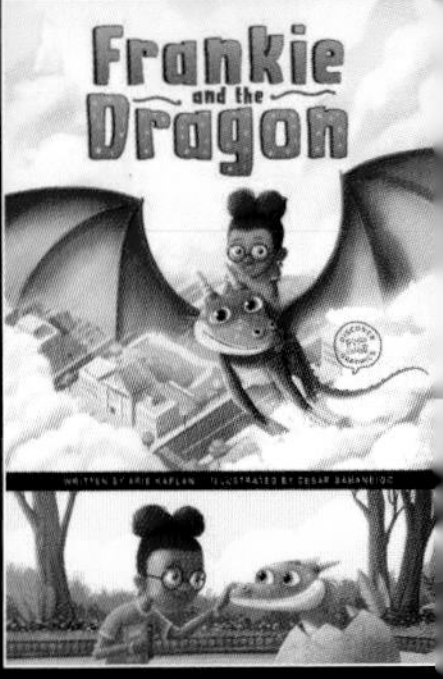
Frankie and the Dragon

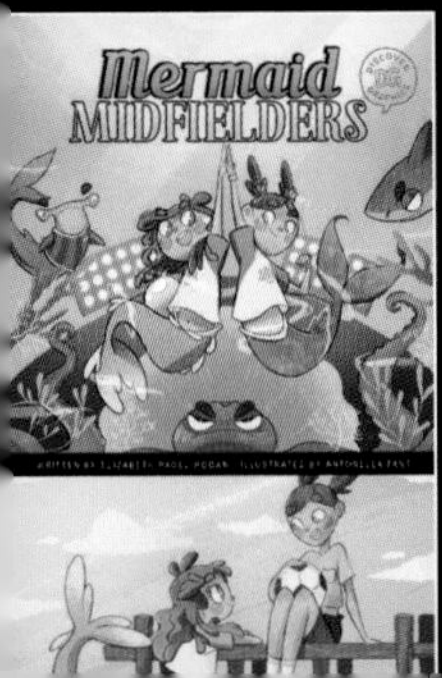
Mermaid MIDFIELDERS

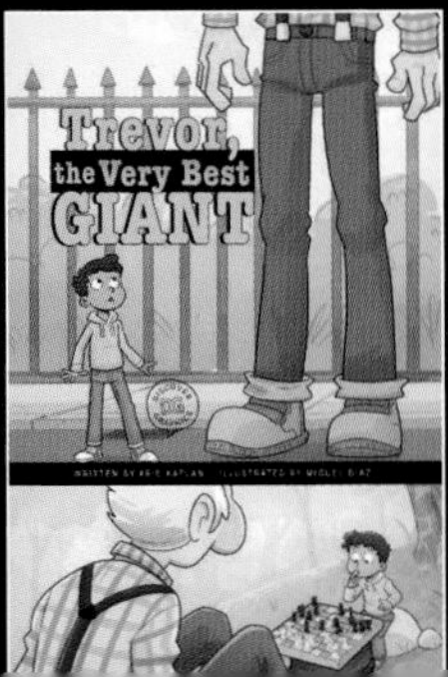
Trevor, the Very Best GIANT

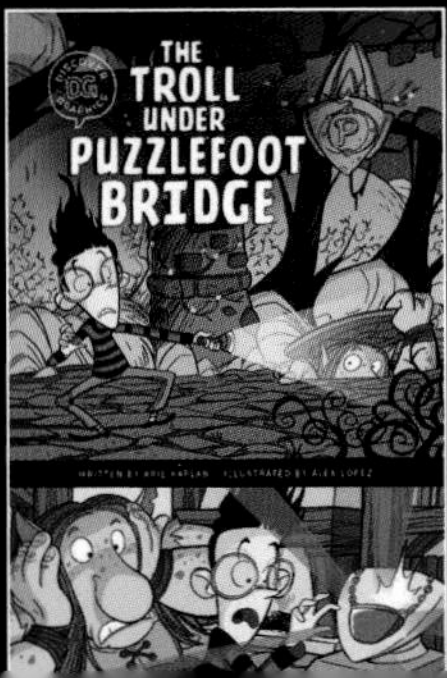
THE TROLL UNDER PUZZLEFOOT BRIDGE

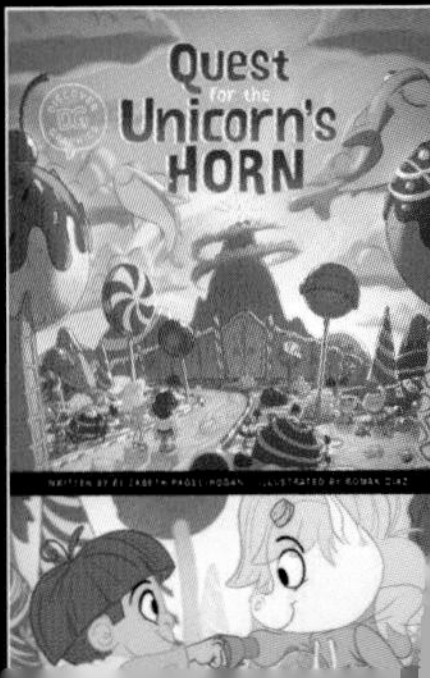
Quest for the Unicorn's HORN

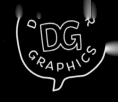

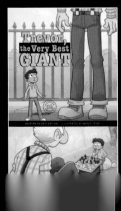